Darl
come ....

Horror Stories
Weird Tales
Flash-Fiction

by
Germano Dalcielo
Elvio Bongorino

If you look in the face of evil,
evil's going to look right back at you.
F. Nietzsche

Where there is much light,
the shadow is deep...
W.Goethe

You die, I survive

"Wake up, sleepyheads! Come on!" He shouted at the two boys, rhythmically clapping his hands.

Aleister jumped against the metal back of his chair. He squinted, blinking his eyes several times at the blinding light of the fluorescent lamp that was dangling a few inches above his head.

"What the f..." He stammered, twisting his mouth into a grimace of disgust. Eventually, he managed to focus on the figure who had just spoken. It was a man wearing a pair of worn suspenders and a pair of weird knickerbockers. The boy addressed him sharply: "Who the hell are you?"

Instinctively, he tried to lean forward, but his arms – flabby and dangling along his hips – did not

7

respond to his commands. He tried to stand up, but even his legs gave no sign of reaction. "Why can't I move? What happened to me?"

Stuart was sitting opposite Aleister on the same line of the floor, still struggling to "unravel the fog". He just muttered: "What time is it? I'm not feeling very well..." He added after drooling a bit of saliva. "By the way, who are *you*?"

"You're finally awake, guys!" – The stranger spoke again, turning around their chairs – "We're running out of time and I must give you some bad news right away: *one of you is going to die*. I know, I know, it sucks but... what are you going to do?" He pretended to shield himself, shrugging his shoulders. He raised his hands in a theatrical gesture. "Accounting issues, so to speak..."

"Excuse me?!"

"What? Is this a joke?" – Aleister was already trying to set himself free – "Did you drug me somehow?"

"The thing is" – The man spoke again without noticing the interruption – "I don't want to decide all by myself. I leave you alone half an hour, so you can think about a bunch of reasons why you should be kept alive. Who will be more original and compelling wins, ok?"

"Whaaat?" Stuart reached a slight falsetto, goggling at the same time.

"Oh, yes, I forgot this one: if I were you, I would not waste the next thirty minutes trying to escape! See you later, buddies!" The weird man exclaimed, wrinkling his nose and snapping his suspenders. He looked quite satisfied and excited. A second later, he disappeared behind a heavy door in the far corner of the room.

"Ok, guys, nice joke! Now, show yourselves, come on!" Aleister shouted. He sounded quite amused, after all.

"Who are you talking to?" Stuart asked him. His voice was broken by nervousness.

"Clearly, this is a joke by my college mates!"

"If this is the case, what have I got to do with it? I don't know you! We're not attending the same school, you jerk!" Stuart shouted in frustration.

"Screw you!"

They both kept staring at the heavy door for endless seconds, waiting. From the outside, there came no noise, nor did voices or chuckles. Aleister swallowed a couple of times. His salivation was out of control.

"Oh no..." It was Stuart to break the silence first.
"What?"

"They were talking about this on the internet..."
"About what?"

"Recently, kidnappers have been abducting two people at a time. After killing one of them, they

9

send evidence to the family of the one who's still alive – usually an ear, a thumb, whatever – threatening to kill him, too. This scares the crap out of the parents. They'll pay the ransom without even blinking an eye. Oh, no, it can't be happening..."

"Bullshit!"

"Didn't you hear what he said? One of us is going to die! He drugged us... accounting issues... Oh my God, everything fits!"

"It's impossible. My parents are not that rich..." Aleister declared with conviction. He took a look around all over the room, twisting his neck and peeking behind his shoulders.

They were sitting on a small circular hatch, which was embossed on the floor. Stuart tried to step aside with a sudden stroke of his pelvis, but the chair did not move an inch. The tiles on the walls were white and aseptic, nearly six feet high. In the far corner opposite the door, there was a long steel sink. The whole room was dotted with exhaust vents and drainage culverts.

"It looks like a slaughterhouse."

"Or a sort of refrigerated room."

"Are you sure?" Aleister asked Stuart, starting to embrace the scenario the boy had suggested.

"I don't know. I hope I will be wrong so bad... Maybe it's really a joke."

"Or, worse than that, we have ended up in some snuff movie..."

"I can't see any cameras, though..." Stuart objected.

They kept silent again for several seconds. The only thing that could be heard was the muffled splash of drops falling from the faucet into the sink.

"What's your name?"

"Stuart. Yours?"

"Aleister. Aleister Huskin."

Their heart beating, pounding in their very ears, would cover any other possible noise.

"I'm scared. I don't want to die!" – Stuart couldn't help but burst into tears – "How can you find a compelling reason not to get killed? In half an hour?!"

"Do not ask *me*..."

The fluorescent light above their heads began buzzing, and a second later, a LED seemed to burn out, just to blink on again, intermittently.

"What are you thinking about?"

"How the hell he got to kidnap me..." Aleister replied, frowning. "I remember being at the Omega Tau initiation party, in the fraternity hall. I had just passed their entry test, by gulping beer right from the hose without catching my breath. I was driving back home. I turned on the radio, raised the volume and then... there is a blank spot in my memories. He must have taken me by surprise, the bastard. Most likely, he was lying in the back seats of my car..."

"You're right! I haven't figured it out myself. The last thing I remember is that I was at Lake George with my family, taking a swim. My mom was sunbathing and my dad was fishing. After that, nothing... I'm sure I was wearing a swimsuit. Why are we wearing this white tank top, instead?"

"How can I know? It's cold in here, by the way... Eh uh, can you hear us?" – Aleister asked the void, looking somewhere upwards – "Get us some clothes, you fucking pervert!"

In that very moment, the door swung open and the man who was holding them hostage stepped into the room, performing a theatrical slide on the floor. He stopped between the two chairs, fiddling with his suspenders. Then he started pacing back and forth, occasionally crossing his arms. In the end, he broke the silence with a straight question: "So what? Have you made up your minds?"

"Half an hour has already elapsed? No way!" Aleister protested.

"Time is relative, son, and so is human life..." The man replied with a wink.

"Wait, wait, please! Don't do this" – Stuart was begging him – "I'm just a kid!"

"I already told you, *kid*: accounting issues! That's it..."

"If it all comes to money, ask both our families for a ransom first!"

"It's more complicated than you could ever get, son. Do not waste your breath!" The man interrupted him, overwhelming his voice.

"You nasty bastard!"

"Many people call me that!" He said, shrugging his shoulders. "Nuff said; time is running out! Each of you, tell me at least a couple of reasons why you deserve to be spared. Come on, surprise me!"

"You can't be serious... I'm only seventeen years old. Damn it!"

"Tick tock, tick tock! You go first, Aleister..." – The kidnapper encouraged him after pulling a mini hourglass out of his vest pocket – "One minute from now: go!"

"What? Wait, wait... Ok... I want to live because... yeah sure, I wish I could change this lousy society and make the world a better place! I will stand for elections. People will remember me as someone who really made the difference. I'm not supposed to die now, ok? I've got a lot of plans for my future! Kill *him*..."

"Well well well... I like you, sooo bluntly! Bravo! Now, it's your turn, Stuart... Stuart?"

The boy was keeping his head down, in embarrassment. His mouth felt kneaded, just like when he could not find the words in front of his classmates and he would end up stuttering. He moistened his lips and, still keeping his eyes fixed on his feet, he spoke in a very low voice:

"I could not think of one single reason why you should choose me. I have no plans for my future. I don't even know what I really want to do as soon as I turn eighteen. My parents have been planning my whole life for the last fifteen years: private schools, conservatory, horse riding, golf... without ever asking me what I really want or if I am happy at all. What should I live for? Becoming the first violin in New York City Orchestra? Being the youngest rider to win the showjumping competition? Or for the golf Master Cup? Pfff!" – Stuart snorted with a disgusted expression on his face – "None of these sounds like a compelling reason to make you save *me* and kill *him*. You better kill *me*..."

"Oh ho, I really couldn't see that coming! It's even better than I thought... You definitely make this easier for me!" The man admitted, pulling out a kind of remote control with two large red buttons. These were intended to trigger the hatch opening. "So... this is it!" He announced triumphantly.

Stuart closed his eyes, waiting for the kidnapper to push the button. Oddly, he was not afraid of sinking down into the hatch. Suddenly, he felt adrenaline wake up his every muscle and flood his every fiber. And yet, something – a kind of ethereal and impalpable force – was still immobilizing him. In the meantime, Aleister was gloating, prey to euphoria, repeating to himself in a whisper: "Yes, yes, I'm safe; I'm fucking safe..."

"And the winner is..." The man recited by raising the remote control as if it was a trophy.

"Noooo!"

Stuart flung open his eyes at hearing that inhuman scream. Aleister's chair was not in its spot anymore. The fluorescent light was barely illuminating the sidewalls of a black square into the floor. The depth of the well could be easily guessed by the horrifying length of the echo. Stuart would swear it was not going to fade away.

"Why? Why the fuck did you do that? I told you to pick meee!" – Stuart shouted at the man. His chest was jumping up and down – "You bastard! He was just a kid!"

"Let's say I like classical music and hate politics instead." The kidnapper replied with a smile. "Now go; you're running out of time."

"Excuse me?"

"I said go! You're free; don't have me repeat it twice!"

"But..."

"Hurry! See the door? Move, before I have second thoughts..."

"What about the ransom? The money? I saw your face... How can you let me go free, knowing that the police is going to take you into custody?"

"Oh, son, that's the last thing in the world that could trouble me at all. By the way, they would not believe you! Trust me! So what? Do I need to kick your ass to get you out of here?"

Stuart got on his feet with some difficulty. Even if he was not well balanced yet, he walked to the door as fast he could.

"As weird as this may sound, thanks... I mean it."

The moment he pushed the handle down, he was blasted by a blinding light.

Presbyterian Hospital,
New York City, NY

"V-fib, no pulse. SATS are dropping!" Nurse Anderson announced to Dr. Farming, who was on duty in the emergency room that afternoon.

"How long has it been?"

"Twenty minutes by now." She replied without raising her eyes. She was focusing on rhythmically pressing the *Ambu*, in order to pump oxygen into the patient's trachea.

"How long has he been underwater?" The doctor asked the boy's mother, who was standing on the ER threshold. She was tapping her mouth with her hands in full turmoil.

"I don't know... I lost sight of him just for one second! I got closer to the shoreline and called him aloud. He wouldn't answer. When I saw the bubbles come to the surface, I jumped into the lake... I blew air in his mouth, trying to make him cough. No way. He was not responsive at all... Oh God, please! Please save him, I'm begging you!"

"What about on the ambulance? Has he ever regained consciousness?"

"Paramedics said he gave no sign of reaction." Was Miss Anderson's only answer.

"Let's try one last time. Push another epi and charge the paddles to 300! Clear!" Dr. Farming shouted to make sure the nurse would raise her hands up, away from the operating table. She triggered the defibrillator while keeping her eyes fixed on the monitor. Unfortunately, the ECG line stayed flat.

"Charge to 360!"

She was staring at the display and the nurse was adding conductive gel on the paddles, when a weak, timid, triangular peak came out from the left corner. Another one. One more. And so on.

"We got him back!" Dr. Farming announced proudly. "Give him dopamine and monitor oxygen values. Keep me posted every fifteen minutes!" She ordered as she rushed outside the room to save other lives.

The boy's mother asked Miss Anderson if she was allowed to enter and get closer to talk to her son. The nurse agreed but she recommended not straining the patient too much. He needed to rest and regain strength. Then she left them alone.

"Stuart, honey, it's mom. Can you hear me? Say something..."

Stuart opened his eyes very slowly, trying to focus on the voice he had just heard. He raised his right hand to his mouth and pulled the oxygen mask aside, in order to make himself hear better. His voice was a bit hoarse.

"Mom..."

"Yes, sweetie, I'm right here. It's ok, don't worry! Everything is going to be fine. You went underwater and you swallowed, right? We're on holiday at Lake George, remember? Oh honey, you scared the hell out of me!"

"Mom..."

"Yes, yes, I'm here. Tell me!"

"*God likes classical music!*"

"Yeah sure, he certainly does. You need to rest now. Why don't you close your eyes and try to sleep? You'll be fine, I promise."

"No, mom, you don't get it!" Stuart interrupted her abruptly. He could not help but smile – "I saw God, I talked to him! He's responsible for sending me back. I was dead, wasn't I? How long have I been dead?"

"I don't know, honey. You're scaring me! You need to rest, please! You're here with me now; this is the only thing that matters. I'll go talk to the doctors. See you upstairs in a while, ok?" His mother pretended to smile in encouragement. Deep down, she was afraid that oxygen deprivation had irrevocably undermined his son's brain functionality.

"He likes music!" – Stuart kept repeating, still laughing out loud. He was re-living the whole scene in his mind – "And he's wearing suspenders!" His chest was bouncing up and down at every cough shot. "Son of a bitch!"

"Oh God... Doctor, doctor!" His mum screamed for help and ran outside the emergency room.

The following day, the local newspapers published the news of a seventeen-year-old boy's tragic death. He was the victim of a car crash for driving under the influence of alcohol.

The paramedics who rushed to the accident scene had tried CPR but unfortunately, the young boy died during transportation to the nearest Hospital.

Stuart Acclestone became the youngest first violin in the New York Philharmonic Orchestra. Regularly, he stops by the Green Wood Cemetery to visit Aleister Huskin's grave.

Big Brother is on my floor

It has been two months by now. I haven't been sleeping, going out or even shaving. I'm spying, that's it. The problem is I like it. I like it a lot.

It happened one day. It was an ordinary morning. Just out of nowhere, I overheard an annoying noise, as if someone was repeatedly hitting the baseboard on our floor. Therefore, I just went to the door to see what the hell was going on.

Today, it is exactly five months that I've been living in my apartment here in SoHo, New York City. On my own. I just couldn't stand living with my parents any longer. My mum is suffering from obsessive-compulsive disorder and, as a result, she was a little too apprehensive; my dad is a drunk who farts and sleeps all day long. This is the reason why, when I turned twenty-nine, I decided to go look for a one-room apartment, one of those already furnished and possibly at a cheap price. I couldn't afford a rent in New York City residential area; my salary at FullTilt customer service wouldn't even cover the first ten days.

Finally, I found a room in this giant 16-floor palace in Canal Street; unfortunately, this neighborhood is not highly recommended. It didn't matter: seven hundred dollars sounded an affordable price to me, especially after the ones I was offered throughout the day. In Manhattan, one-room rentals hardly stay under one thousand bucks.

Actually, I must admit that I have liked this tiny 32-square-meter space since the first time I saw it.

When the estate agent brought me to take a look at the apartment, I felt a sudden tingling at my stomach: it was not the typical gurgle when you're hungry. It was a feeling of pure excitement instead; it was adrenaline running in my veins for the thrilling sensation of starting a brand new life from that very moment.

This room definitely suited me and had to be mine. I accepted the offer; I paid a refundable two-month deposit and eventually settled in a dozen days later.

The first two months went off smoothly: I would come back home from work at 6.00 p.m.; would stop by MacDonald's to get some burgers and fries; would relax on my couch and watch two CSI Miami episodes in a row. Sometimes, I got so tired that I didn't even open up the bed under the couch; I just fell asleep with the remote control still in my hands, often leaving the TV on. The following morning, I would wake up finding my hands still greasy and the fries box stuck between my neck and my shoulders.

At the beginning, living on your own is kind of exciting. You can do whatever you like: you can turn the volume of the stereo up to its maximum level; walk round completely naked or masturbate in total relaxation (my mum caught me in the act two times when I was a boy); wash dishes whenever you want, watch TV till late at night (my dad would have me pay the utility bill from time to time).

However, after the first weeks, the initial excitement fades away and routine sneaks in. Routine is boring, it's too mechanical. It makes you want to sleep and do nothing else, in the long term. Routine reminds me of that movie where Charlie Chaplin stars a worker in an assembly plant. Every evening, at the time of going back home, he would repeat in the air the same mechanical gestures he had made during his work shift at the assembly line.

Social alienation swallowed me up, too, a couple of months later.

My days were all alike: early in the morning, I would get up, have breakfast, dress up in a rush, run to the subway and get off at Avenue Street; then I would come up to the FullTilt building fourth floor; sit down at my desk, wear ear cuffs and deal with customer complaints and requests. At noon and a half, I would have an hour lunch break. I would go down to the coffee shop on the first floor; have a sandwich and a cup of coffee; go out in the parking place to light a cigarette and pretend to nod in response to some colleague's questions about New York Knicks chances to reach the playoffs.

The hour would pass in a flash; I would go up again to the fourth floor, put my ear cuffs back on, and rattle off the usual common courtesy speech to customers. At 5.00 p.m., I would finally finish my shift and fly home by the subway.

This was my schedule every single day, except on Sundays, which I would spend idling in bed for the most part of the day.

One evening, once I got home, I threw myself down on the couch and rested my head on the pillow. Suddenly, I felt my right auricle aching: *I*

24

still had the call-center ear cuffs on me. All the way home from work, I did not realize I hadn't pulled them off when leaving the office.

I jumped to my feet in no time and threw the ear cuffs against the wall. I had become Charlie Chaplin. I had turned into a FullTilt little robot, damn it!

Alienation, globalization, consumerism had trapped me in their twisted mechanism.

Sorry, I quit. You won't swallow me up.

The following day, I didn't go to work; I called the office on the phone pretending I was sick. I needed time to think. I needed to pull myself together and take control of my life again.

I'm in charge... I'm in charge... I kept repeating in my mind.

I stayed out all day long. I didn't care if FullTilt would send an inspector to check if I was really sick. Who cares? I was going to quit that fucking job. No regrets.

I went to the mall, to the movies, to a blind date I had arranged on the internet and to Madison Square Garden for a live concert.

I really enjoyed myself. I did whatever would cross my mind, regardless of time schedules to be respected or quality targets to reach mandatorily. *I was free.* I felt like that for the very first time in my life.

Eventually, at about 7.00 p.m., I went back home; I ate some junkie food and fell asleep on the couch while Horatio Cane was still looking for the murderer. At the beginning, I did not realize that basically, under the surface, nothing had changed. Yes, it is true that I could go out and do whatever I pleased, that I could enjoy myself and my freedom whenever I wanted to, but in the end, what would I do once the money would be over? I quit the job, so all the money I had left was a small part of the two salaries I had earned at FullTilt.

How long would this life last, with barely two thousand dollars to live?

On the sixth day, I didn't have a penny left. To fill the void I was feeling within me, I devoted myself to shopping spree and luxury dinners in high-star restaurants for five days in a row.

Things being like that, I locked myself inside the apartment and watched twelve CSI episodes non-stop, just not to face the gravity of my situation. On the seventh day, I didn't know what to do: I couldn't go out (not having a single buck), and I couldn't stay home either. The house was a mess; I hadn't been doing some cleaning for weeks.

Therefore, when I heard that weird noise coming from the floor of my building – it sounded like someone was kicking the baseboard – I made towards the spy-hole and took a look at the outside. On my floor – the ninth –, there were other five apartments; in the middle, there was the elevator surrounded by the stairs. The noise that was intriguing me was being made by the woman from apartment number 11. She was kicking the baseboard over and over to kill time, waiting for the elevator to reach our floor.

She was about forty years old; she was wearing a pantsuit, one of a weird color purple. She looked well groomed; her hair was all gathered in a pretty *chignon* and both her wrists were dotted with a dozen bracelets. Seeing her so impatient, one would say she was going to have the date or maybe the interview of her life. Honestly, I didn't know her; I hadn't bumped into her since I came to live here. This was due to my unsociable behavior as well as to her never welcoming me.

All the faces and sighs she was doing, as the elevator slowly climbed to our floor, were quite funny. All of a sudden, the doors swung open; just before entering the cabin, she took a good look around to make sure nobody would see her. After that, she put her right hand in her pants to slip the loincloth off from inside her buttocks. Once she was finished doing that, she smiled and vanished into the elevator. She had a satisfied look on her face.

I burst into a sound laugh after leaving my spy-hole spot. It is deeply true that you can't judge a book by its cover. My neighbor had just been the nth proof.

I was washing dishes in the kitchen sink – where a dozen flies had been dwelling by now – when I overheard the typical sound the elevator makes the very moment it arrives at a floor. So I ran to the spy-hole to take a peek again.

This time, was the turn of the pensioner from flat number 14, the middle one. He was carrying a trash bag and wearing a hat on his head, which was almost pulled down on his eyes. A fisherman jacket would barely button up on his prominent belly. When the elevator doors opened, he raised his right leg in a statuesque pose and farted so loud that the noise echoed all over the floor and through the stairwell. I burst out into a wild laugh but I shut my mouth immediately to prevent him from noticing my presence behind the door. The old man looked well pleased; in fact, he was still smiling. Eventually, he toddled into the cabin as nothing ever happened.

I couldn't believe my own eyes. Where the hell had I got to?

Still unbelieving, I got back to washing dishes. Fifteen minutes later, I found myself stuck to the spy-hole. *Again.*

On the floor, was standing the boy from flat number 13. Apparently, he was coming back home from school – I can't say if primary or junior high school. He was short; his back was slightly curved under the weight of his bag, which was crammed full of books. He was wearing a pair of jeans, which were too long on the ankles by the way, and a pair of rough trekking-shoes. I could easily see him hesitating in front of the elevator, slowly pulling his gloves off. All of a sudden, he put a finger in his nose and stuck the bogey on the call button. After that, he rushed to his flat, pushing the ring bell furiously, and waiting for somebody to open and let him in.

I couldn't believe what I had just seen. What kind of freaking people were my neighbors? How could I be the only one behaving decently? I must admit something despite myself: I was having a lot of fun.

An hour later, was the turn of the "witch" from flat number 15. This weird old woman in her sixties had rough white hair and a deviated septum, which made her nose look like a hook. She would never go out without a saltshaker. She would stand on her flat threshold, haphazardly throwing salt on her doormat and the marble tiles all around.

I was not able to read her lips from behind my door, but I'm pretty sure she was pronouncing some odd, ritual prayers in order to throw negative bad energies away. After a couple of minutes, she would call for the elevator and disappear. Maybe she was going to some witches meeting, or only God knows where.

The following days, I would run to the spy-hole at the least noise. One morning, the cleaning woman was working on our floor. She was using her mop in lazy slowness all over the tiles. Every now and then, she would stop and blow her nose with a tiny tissue; then she would put it in her apron again, which she was wearing tied around her waist. I felt sorry for her. She looked like someone who had just gone through a romantic setback or some love woes.

Her nemesis was the slut from flat number 16. In the last three months, I have always caught her as she sneaks into the lawyer's flat number 12, as soon as his wife goes to work. One day, I was stuck to the spy-hole, peeking. I was wondering when she would sneak out. She showed up forty minutes later, looking relaxed and fully satisfied, with a 32-tooth smile on her face.

My neighbors have really turned out to be nasty people.

In the meantime, days went by. Spying had become my daily routine, my hobby, the compensation for my existential void. I didn't even realize that, although I had fought so much to avoid involvement in society and work alienation, I was finding myself trapped in the even more devious alienation that was starring on my floor every day.

All this until the day I saw the estate agent again. Yes, the same one who helped me find this flat five months ago. She walked out of the elevator, preceded by her own perfume, which had slipped under my very door. She looked as beautiful as five months before; she was still tanned and dressed to kill. Her hair was streaked and she was wearing a pair of fashion black boots and a white shirt, purposely kept half-open on her chest. She was followed by two young people, a girl and a boy in their thirties, clearly engaged. They wanted to go live together so they had asked the estate agent to help them find an apartment.

"Let's see... Every time, I can't remember which one it is..."

I can perfectly hear her from behind my door as she speaks.

"Oh, here it is! Come over, guys!" She says to the fiancés in an enthusiastic tone. I can see her pulling a couple of keys out of her pocket. She makes towards my door. *Oh Ho... What is she going to do?*

Fuck! When I hear her turn the key in the keyhole, it's already too late. I step back and shout: "What the hell do you think you're doing? This is private property; you're committing housebreaking!" Unfortunately, the door opening wide interrupts me abruptly.

"Excuse me?! Why do you still have my keys? I rent this room five months ago! Hello? Do you copy? This one is already rented!" I scream in her face but she doesn't even consider me. "God damn it! Will you answer me? Can't you see I'm right here?!"

Her only answer is the same smart speech she has already rattled off five months ago, in order to talk me into renting the apartment.

"It's sunny, airy, and quite habitable even if it's just a single room. It's lovely, bright, already furnished... What do you want more? At just three hundred bucks, it's impossible to find something better! So, what do you think?" She asked the two lovebirds, who were devouring the flat with their eyes.

"Whaaat? You bitch, I'm right here! Are you fucking kidding me? I live hereeee! That's enough! I'm sick of you. Get the hell out of here!" I shout in her face. I'm definitely losing my nerve.

"Is it true that two months ago, the guy who lived here hung himself in the shower? This is why the owner is renting it out at this low price, huh? It's because nobody wants to lease it... Would you tell us if the house was haunted, wouldn't you?" The girl asks the agent, chewing her lower lip out of nervousness.

"Do not mind newspapers and gossip! Isn't it lovely?" She is trying to veer off.

I don't want to believe it. I *can't* believe it. I try to swallow but I can't feel my Adam's apple. I yell again but they don't hear me. They *can't* hear me. They can't see me. I want to run, get out of here, just go somewhere else. Just out. I rush to the door, which is still open, but on the threshold, an invisible barrier knocks me down to the floor. I stand up and make another attempt, but there's nothing I can do. I can't go out. *They* won't let me.

This flat, which was the natural habitat to my antisocial behavior during my lifetime and where I relegated myself away from the outside world, has now become my personal Purgatory. All my life, I have metaphorically closed the doors to people; I was careless of everything and everybody; so now, my purgative punishment is to see my neighbors live their lives through a glass, in a coercive, undignified, morbid way.

Isn't it ironic the way God has punished me?

Should I ever meet Him one day, I would definitely want to shake His hand.

The Ouija board

"Tell me what happened, Tyler. Start from the beginning. Try to relax; let your memories go back to that day. Do not be afraid."

Doctor Stanton, a renowned forensic psychiatrist, crossed her legs glibly. She was sitting in her office in Cleveland, Ohio; she looked eager to listen to the story directly from the protagonist, the boy who was lying on the little couch in front of her.

"Five of us came up with the idea of occupying the school that night." Tyler started to speak, staring at some undefined point in the ceiling. "Earlier that day, we had arranged a protest against the public instruction funding cuts, but the police kept pushing us back. At nightfall, we decided to barricade inside the school. We were lying on the couches in the main lobby, talking about this and that. We got terrorized when we realized the possibility of facing the night without anything to get high with. Beer was over; weed would barely be enough for a couple of hours. It was just 11 p.m.: what could we do? Sleep? No way. I had brought some board games from home but, when you are seventeen years old, there are only two things in your mind: the first one – weed – was running out earlier than expected; the second one – sex – was the true reason why Brian, our class representative and my best friend, had invited two cheerios to spend the night shift with us.

In about twelve hours, the school was already a pigpen: some couches were completely torn off; the desks had been turned upside down; most doors unhinged; toilets were waterlogged. We laid our sleeping bags in the north corner of the main lobby, to take advantage of an electric heater in that spot. The central heating was not working, probably on a specific order by our principal.

I coughed a couple of times due to all the smoke I was inhaling and I said: "Why don't we set up a séance? I saw there is a Ouija board in the tool room, down in the basement. What do you think? It could be fun..."

Honestly, I felt a little dazed by weed. I can't even recall how this idea could have possibly crossed my mind. The only thing I know for sure is that I could not imagine my friends would take me seriously. I just threw it out to say something smart. I didn't really mean it.

There were a few seconds of silence, the exact time brain takes to embrace an idea. After that, one of the guys laughed out nervously and eventually, all their heads began nodding, fully convinced.

"Do you want to summon *Beetlejuice*? Maybe a female ghost would suit you better, since you're going to fail to score tonight. You know that, huh?"

"Or maybe... do you want to call Casper and ask him for an autograph?"

Jeremy and Brian were making a fool of me, hinting at my passion for animated cartoons, and taking for granted that the two cheerios would have sex with them exclusively. At that point, I was feeling a bit pissed off, so I decided to challenge them for real. I raised my voice and said: "No, I want to summon some demon, a Jinn hopefully. If you don't have the nerve, we can play Scrabble instead". I had just thrown a far too tempting bait for their egos. Brian and Jeremy could not afford the chance of acting coward in front of the girls. One of them, Cassidy, asked in a whisper: "What is a *uiya* board?"

"It's just a simple wooden, oval-shaped board. There are alphabet letters from A to Z and numbers from 0 to 9. They are screen printed along the edges. In the middle, 'yes' and 'no' are usually highlighted. Basically, you need something to help the summoned spirit with, so that he can communicate with you and be easily understood. You do this with a little pointer, called *planchette*. It looks like a big guitar plectrum. Those who sit around the table during the séance will gently put their fingertips on it, without pushing it. The spirit is the one who moves it to answer the questions, using letters for words and numbers for dates or counts. As long as you don't pee yourself when you see the pointer moving by itself..." I concluded for effect. My goal was to provoke them and string them along – yes, I must admit it was a heavy-handed prank, but I knew no spirit would show up, you know? I would be the only one moving the *planchette*, being careful they would not notice me. In fact, I was supposed to direct the séance, since I was the only one experienced in a dark subject like that.

Actually, I only watched some horror movie where the Ouija board was used, and I only read some blog posts about it on the internet.

Apparently, that was enough to have my friends hang on my every word.

"Who do you think you're talking to?" – Brian spoke again. He sounded definitely hooked – "There is nothing I am afraid of! Let's go for it. It's going be a lot of fun..."

We got down to the basement and entered the room where the gymnasium tools were usually stored. We found the Ouija board on a shelf. It was completely covered with dust. We were feeling so excited when we sat down around the coffee table in the janitors' room! I invited the five of them to gently lay their index fingertips on the edges of the pointer. After that, I finally gave way to my show.

"Now, we make the *planchette* rotate a dozen times in a counterclockwise way, in order to attract the spirit and let him understand we're trying to connect with him – or her. At that point, we will get started. We'll bring the pointer back to the middle of the board and we'll wait for the Jinn to move it – as long as he shows himself, of course. I need to advise you guys, against laughing, panicking, getting hysterical or insulting him, because the demon could get nervous and, as a result, decide to cut down any possible communication. Ask a question one at a time, spelling it slowly. Last but not least, do NOT EVER – I underlined this by making a pause for effect – pull your finger off of the pointer before the séance is over and the spirit is gone on its own volition, or freed by us to go. If you lose the grip on the *planchette*, you will interrupt the bond that ties and holds the demon inside the Ouija board. As a consequence of that, an opening would ensue: a window on our world no spirit would ever miss."

Deep inside, I was laughing my ass off. I could see my friends completely hanging on my every word. They looked at me wide-mouthed in disbelief, as if I had become the coolest person in the whole school in no time.

I made the pointer roll along the board edges for a dozen times; in the end, I re-positioned it between the "yes" and "no", right in the middle. After that, I asked aloud in a pretended, solemn voice tone: "Is there anyone out there?"

If I had manipulated the *planchette* too soon, the guys wouldn't have bought it and my show wouldn't have lasted any longer, not even another minute. In order to make the whole scene believable, I had planned to move the pointer slowly to the "yes" only after the first question had been asked at least three times. The problem is there was no fucking need for it! At the second invitation that I addressed the spirit, with my nose up in the air to fully play my part in the act, the *planchette* began moving unexpectedly on its own, almost slipping on the wood, towards the "yes".

"You're pushing it, Tyler. I can see you." Brian was accusing me of cheating. He hated being fooled, even more in front of two girls.

"No, I'm not moving it, I swear!"

"Tyler, cut it off. It's not funny!"

"I'm telling you it wasn't me! It must be the ideomotor effect they were talking about on the internet. If you think the pointer is going to move eventually, you'll unconsciously cause an unwilling movement".

Actually, I was talking more to myself than to them. My astonishment was sincere. I was trying to find a logical explanation to that unreal situation, which was not supposed to happen.

"Hey, what's going on now?" Cassidy asked, interrupting me abruptly.

The *planchette* had started whirling along the board edges for a few seconds, as if it had gained a spark of life. This was a crystal clear signal: the spirit wanted us to focus on him. He was eager to communicate with us.

Every one of us had his finger grabbed to the pointer not to lose the grip; it was going round and round furiously. Eventually, it went back to the middle. I swallowed up twice, as stunned as I was by the unexpected turn the séance had just taken, and asked in a trembling voice: "W-who are you?"

First, the *planchette* began moving sharply to the A, then diagonally to the Z, again to the A and the Z. I was starting to think it was fooling us, but a couple of seconds later, it whizzed on the E and the L.

"*Azazel*?" I asked the void, not knowing where to look. I was terrified; I was perfectly aware that the whole thing had gotten out of hand. It couldn't be one of the guys moving the pointer as a joke; the name the spirit had just told us was far too plausible and realistic to think it had been made up by one of my friends.

The *planchette* darted to the "yes". The only noise that could be heard in the unreal silence inside the janitors' room, was the deaf rubbing of the wood against the wood.

"Guys, this would be the right moment to tell me this is a joke." Sheldon was sweating. He was about to freak out.

"I'm not moving it, I told you!"

"Shut the hell up, for Christ's sake! It's moving again..."

"A→S→K".

The spirit wanted us to ask him questions. He wanted to connect with us. What the hell could we ask a demon?

"Ehm... Where are you, exactly?" Cassidy had just found the smartest question ever in the meanders of her brain.

"A→M→I→D→S→T".

"Are you amidst us? How? Are you suspended over the table?"

"Are you touching me?" Lexie addressed Brian, who was sitting on her right side, when she felt an imperceptible caress on her hip.

"No, I'm not. Why?"

"Take your dirty hands off of me! Now!" She ordered him, slightly jumping on the chair.

"I'm not touching you... I swear!"

"So, who's fucking doing it? Whoever it is, stop! Now! It's not funny at all. Sheldon, is it you?"

"I have my hands on the table, see?"

"Oh God, again!" She shouted, almost freaking out.

The *planchette* solved the mystery once and for all.

"N→I→C→E→P→A→N→T→I→E→S".

"Go to hell, you assholes!" Lexie's face turned red. Unthinkingly, she got to her feet.

"Nooo! What the fuck have you done? I told you not to pull your finger off, for no reason at all!" I yelled at her, bringing my left hand to my forehead in distress. I was desperate; I knew exactly what her behavior would be responsible for.

"I don' t give a shit. I quit! Do you really think I will stay here and let you make fool of me?". She left the room slamming the door with a slap.

In the meantime, the pointer had flown to letters T and Y in a flash.

"Thank you? What for?" Cassidy asked stupidly.

The Jinn had reached his goal.

"N→O→W→U→D→I→E".

At that very moment, panic got the best of us. I still couldn't believe this was really happening, or that I had really summoned a demon. I hoped it was just a nightmare. I was probably asleep, or completely drunk; alternatively, I had likely passed out for inhaling too much weed. I wished it was that way so bad...

"Please wait! Let's talk! Stay here with us... Please wait! We've been respectful. Do not leave..."

"2→L→A→T→E".

The table started vibrating by itself as if it was electrified. A second later, the door swung open, making us jump on the chairs: on the threshold, barely illuminated by the hall light, Lexie was hanging two feet from the floor, as if an invisible force was holding her suspended in the air.

It was not supposed to go this way; it was meant to be just a joke, a fucking prank among fellas... Jesus Christ, I didn't want to summon a monster!"

"Calm down, Tyler. Go on. What happened next?" Doctor Stanton asked, with an unabashed look on her face.

"Lexie's neck was smoking! We could clearly hear the crackling of burning flesh over her screams... oh God... I will never forget that. I didn't do it on purpose; I could not imagine a demon would come out of a damn wooden board!"

"Easy, Tyler, take it easy! Breathe; let go of the stress. Do you remember seeing anybody behind the girl? Focus on your memory; close your eyes. Try to re-live that moment. I know this is hard and scary, but you're safe now. No one can hurt you, I promise."

"There was no man, Doctor. The police won't believe me; nobody wants to fucking believe me: neither do you. The Jinn was holding our friend up in the air and he incinerated her neck in only one second. How many times will I have to repeat this? It just looked like spontaneous human combustion – well, if you do not take into account the acceleration with witch it was occurring! After a few seconds, Lexie fell onto the floor. We could clearly see her neck bone completely exposed. There was no blood; it had instantly coagulated, just like when you cauterize a bleeding injury. It was a hell of a hole; it was disgusting! After that, I only remember Cassidy screaming; people trying to break the window to get out of there; objects and stuff flying from all over the shelves; the table turning upside down; the Ouija board fluctuating in the air as if it was alive... I couldn't see all this coming. I couldn't foresee anything like that. They all died because of me. He's going to come pick me up, too. He won't let me go; he won't leave me alone until he finds me. Doctor Stanton, please help me! You have to believe me!"

"I believe you, Tyler. Do not panic. Take it easy; breathe."

Doctor Stanton was lying in order to calm the patient down. She was not buying the whole story, of course. She lowered her eyes on the file she was holding upon her thighs. Tyler had already been diagnosed by her FBI colleague with a delusional, hallucinatory state of mind. Doctor Stanton was going to countersign the document.

"Try to relax, Tyler; close your eyes. How did you get to save yourself and escape?"

"I guess I have to thank the internet and all the online urban legends." The boy answered promptly. "Above the cupboard in the janitors' room, there was a couple of salt packages. I frantically opened up one of them and sewed the salt all over on the floor around me, making up a continuous circle. Demons cannot trespass it; salt is a powerful protector and purifier. I told Brian to rush toward me and get inside the circle, but he didn't make it... Oh God, please forgive me! He killed them all... He killed all my friends!"

"It was not your fault, Tyler."

"After that, I called 911. The police arrived twenty minutes later. The Jinn must have left; I presumed that from the fact the police officers were staying alive. They handcuffed me, assuming I was responsible for the murders. I didn't want to leave the circle for any reason in the world; I couldn't be certain that bastard was really gone. I asked the officer for a couple of pure iron-made handcuffs – iron is another element that keeps demons away – and I picked up from the floor all the salt I managed to gather in my hands. Once we got to the police station, I asked to be questioned in a cell, behind iron bars. A few hours later, they let me go free. The coroner confirmed the deaths were due to an abnormal, unknown combustion process, not scientifically explainable; something that a 17-year-old boy could not have committed.

The police is not buying the summoning story and won't protect me. I am scared, Doctor. I don't want to die... I have to go around with crucifixes, holy water phials, and salt in my pockets... Please! I know they have made me come here for a psychiatric evaluation, but you need to write that I'm telling the truth. It's not my fault! It was supposed to be a joke; I didn't do it on purpose. I didn't want my friends to die, God strike me dead! You have to believe me. I'm not crazy!"

"Ok, ok, everything is going to be fine, Tyler. Take a long, deep breath. That's enough for today. Let's arrange for Tuesday, next week, same hour. Now, I am going to prescribe you something that will help you sleep better, ok?"

"It'll turn out to be ineffective. I haven't been able to sleep for days... As soon as I close my eyes, I can see them dying in front of me... over and over again..."

"Trust me; you will get to sleep with this drug." Dr. Stanton assured him. She got up to her feet and reached her desk to write down the prescription. "I recommend you use this medicine responsibly; pour just twenty drops – at the most – in a glass of water, ok?" She said, as she was intent on writing the appropriate dosage.

"Doctor?"

"Yes?"

"We never sleep."

The psychiatrist turned back. The sudden, cavernous voice tone of the boy had stunned her with all its load of evil. Unfortunately, it was too late for her. Tyler had grabbed her jaws with only one hand, squeezing her neck in an inextricable grip. Using a superhuman strength, he was holding her suspended one foot from the floor. She tried to call for help, but her vocal cords ended up carbonized in a few seconds. The last image this world granted Melanie Stanton's irises, was her last patient, who was watching her die. His head was slightly inclined to the right, and his eyes, reduced to two ellipsoidal holes, were staring at his macabre, pyrotechnical show.

Tyler Hastings jumped to number 4 in the FBI list of most wanted criminals in the United States of America. In the following weeks, after other burned bodies were found in the near States of Indiana and Michigan, the Federal Bureau passed the case over to the Interpol. They felt resigned to classify it as an X-file.

Calandrina

The lady was always cold. Her face was pale, livid and elusive-featured. It looked powdered with heliotrope dust. This is why I nicknamed her Calandrina, like the invisible character in an Italian novella I once read at school.

She had arrived in November, along with the bad weather, the rain and boredom. I became interested in her in the first place because of that vague, indefinite, fog-like look she had. What was she doing in the apartment during her stay? What about when she got out?

Every night, I would see her alone and seemingly lost in thought. She would stand for hours behind the glass of the only window that overlooked the courtyard.

Calandrina was definitely different from any other creature I had ever observed. Every night, she would stand at the window for an endless time. Behind her, only pitch dark. I could guess her presence because that impossible face of hers looked illuminated by her own white eyes. At some point, she would bend her head, as if she wanted to lean a bit forward; then she would bring her hands to her mouth as if she was going to pray. She would just puff air into them, in order to warm them up a little more.

Sometimes, I felt like she was looking at me. She would remain that way three or four more minutes, sniffing the night. Then she would retire quietly into the silence of her room.

During the day, she would rarely go out. I could rather see her after sunset, but she would stay outside only momentarily. Every now and then, someone came to visit her. Each time, it was someone different, any age, and any class. No one, though, brought children along. They usually stayed inside the house for about an hour, and eventually left. Many of them looked unsettled. Their faces were stiffened. Their eyes were glossy and bloodshot, as if they had just cried. They walked away slowly. They seemed hampered by unseen forces or overwhelming burdens, hard to drag by.

Just once, a woman was smiling when she closed Calandrina's door. She looked dreamy and dazed. She was young and blonde. She kept kissing the little medallion she was carrying around her neck.

***

"Who is it?"
"It's me."
"Me who?"
"..."
"What's your name?"
"Albert."
"Why are you here, Albert?"
"I don't know. I want to talk to you, I guess... Can I come in?"

Calandrina showed me a wicker chair in the middle of the room, right next to her bed. A dark, greenish atmosphere made everything hardly perceivable. It felt like I had merged, with my eyes wide open, into a murky pool of seaweed and salt water. I could hardly distinguish her profile. She was standing, illuminated by the flickering light of a candle on the corner table. She was the only one breathing in the room. The air was so thickened with nightmares that I could even see them whirling in filaments around her slender, clear figure. It looked like they wanted to touch Calandrina's hair with their long fangs.

She was still pointing her arm at the wicker chair. She kept staring at me, silently. Her lips had become a black, fuzzy spot.

"Sure, take a seat! How old are you?"
"I'm thirteen years old, nearly fourteen."
"Do you know why you are here?"
"I want to talk to you."
"Ok, let's talk."

She was perfectly calm, even though a thin, strident veil was interspersing the sound of her words. In one corner of her soul, she was alarmed.

"Albert, you know you should not be here, don't you?"
"N-no... I can't see why not. I have been watching you for months. You are *weird*."
"Oh yes, I know that... I am well aware of being weird." She smiled in a friendly manner. "And not just for those like you."

What a dialogue! I felt shaken like a little fish in some frying oil.

"Your place is somewhere else. I can help you, as long as you follow my instructions."

"So tell me; I'm all ears..."

I made up a smile on my face, the best smile that could come to my mind.

"What were you doing before meeting me?"

Oh no... This question cut my brain open as if it was a blade. I felt pain from head to toe. I wanted to lie down on the floor, roll over, reach out, scream, scratch, yell...

She kept sitting tight. She was looking at me, warming her hands up by blowing all over them and hugging herself in her heavy sweater. I don't know what color it was. All of a sudden, she stood up and came closer to me. The air all around had taken a wooly, stifling texture.

"How did it happen?"

"I have been kidnapped."

"What do you remember?"

"He grabbed me. I was coming back home after the piano lesson. I had just left Professor Diego's house. Do you know him?"

"Yes I do. I see him around pretty often." Calandrina smiled and looked upwards as if expecting my teacher's shape to appear on the ceiling. "He lives two blocks from here. Who kidnapped you?"

"It was a man. I don't know his name. He pulled over and asked me something about... I don't know; I can't recall anymore."

Suddenly, I burst out into tears. Making no noise, though, no hiccups. The more I tried to remember, the more the darkness would choke and clutch my mind, preventing me from recalling.

After that, there was a throbbing pain in my neck. It was deep and overwhelming. I felt myself slammed against the wall by an invisible force. I collapsed on the floor like a deflated balloon, pressing my hands onto my belly. It felt like I was being hit by a row of powerful and unceasing kicks.

"Help me!"

"Do not worry. Those are your last memories. Let go of them. You are beyond, now..."

"What? I feel so bad, please help me!"

"I am helping you, indeed. Come over to me... Why do you call me Calandrina?" She pronounced this name in a sweet, low voice, in the same tone moms use to tell their babies some made-up fairytales. How could she know that I was calling her that? "My name is Ilvia..." She added calmly.

"I call you Calandrina because you are so subtle and white that you look almost invisible. Like a shadow. One could think that you are able to hide yourself using the powers of a magic stone. This reminds me of a novella our Professor used to read for us..."

"Albert, come over to me. Can you see this?"

Yes, I could. It was a bright, yellow sphere, which had a pulsing "peanut" on the inside. She was showing it to me by lifting it over the middle of her chest. Suddenly, I felt a strong, attractive power coming from that. I took a step toward her.

"Do not stop. Do not be afraid of what is going to happen when you touch it."

I kept walking. All the anguish, fear and pain flooding over me in those last moments, were taking a new direction now. They were taking leave from me. That restless peanut was saying a faint, almost imperceptible "hi" to me, guiding me to a remote little spot: a colorless, yet friendly, note.

***

"Hi, Albert. Your mom and dad love you very much. And so do I."

Ilvia put a bunch of daisies right next to the huge stone jar, which was already filled with white carnations.

"He was arrested yesterday. He has killed eight more children since you died. I need to go now."

She stepped back, peeping at the small watch on her wrist. Then she smiled, and her eyes focused on somewhere else. There was a rarefied atmosphere all around, with blinding rays of light every now and then. Silent birds could be heard in the background, as they rustled among the wet pine boughs. A sharp ear could also catch the trampling of some widow's footsteps, the giggle of a faraway child and the chill of the shadows, which were waiting behind the hedges.

"I have an appointment with your piano teacher at three o'clock. He is coming round every day by now. He wants to question the tarots, to find out if he will ever meet another girlfriend."

Ilvia slightly shook her head. Thinking about the piano teacher made her blush. He looked handsome and a bit weird, though. He used to walk in a bizarre way and had a funny, unmistakable voice. "You have a... *priestly* voice!" She had told him with a smile on her face, as he tried to woo her in front of a coffee shop. At first, he was a bit offended; then he kept performing his innocent, clumsy witticisms, so that Ilvia ended up accepting his invitation for a cup of coffee.

"I know that he doesn't believe in these "things" at all. Sometimes, he stares at me in a smugly way, as if he had to deal with a crazy woman who needs to be indulged. He is stopping by only because now he feels fine again. He doesn't know that I will be the next one. I'm not going to tell him. He will find it by himself tonight, when he drives back home. Tomorrow, he will come again to visit me, bringing me one of his favorite books as a gift. On the first page, I will find a nice dedication, informing me that he is totally mine by now, unconditionally."

Ilvia's eyes whirled around as if she was already figuring out the scene.

"I will be the next and the last one."

Her smile faded away on her lips. They bent downwards in full sadness.

"I wish I could escape the inevitable. I wish I could hide myself behind a magic stone that could make me invisible to sorrow and pain. The worst side of my condition is to be destined to suffer misfortunes well in advance. Eleven months from now, I will be losing him."

She covered her eyes with one of her hands, as if she wanted to hold something too ugly away from the world, something that only she could already see.

"Albert, I wish you could do me a special favor: will you come to pick him up when it is his turn? I won't be able to help him like I did with you. Please promise me."

A second later, it started snowing. A few frost corianders began whirling around her head, as agitated by a flutter of invisible wings. Ilvia cupped her hands near her face, to warm them by blowing air right in the middle.

"I promise."

Ring around the rosie...

Dragan Iliescu inhaled avidly from the tiny butt he was holding between his fingertips, hoping the smoke would reach his lungs deep down to the very alveolus. Despite the sunny, 60-degree morning, he had been feeling cold since the moment he got out of his van.

He stopped in front of the enormous, Victorian-style gate, waiting. In that point, the air felt different, as if it was suspended. A thin fog was surrounding the building along the outside wall; it cleared at first-floor level and completely melt away at the top-floor windows.

The gate had been left half-open, and was slightly oscillating. The hinges were squeaking, making some sort of a creepy sound. For just a couple of seconds, the strident noise sounded like a dragged yawn.

The burning sensation at his fingertips reminded Dragan that the dilly-dallying time was over. He had to make up his mind and go inside.

He had taken the job almost by necessity: the building industry had been recently going through a hard recession overall – not to mention his own firm, which was on the edge of bankruptcy.

Ten years earlier, he had left Romania to seek his fortune. Eventually, he settled in Ferrara, Italy, working as a simple bricklayer before starting his own building business. At the beginning, everything seemed to go smoothly, but in the last period, taxes, delayed payments, competition and the big drop of the housing market itself had been taking the wind out of his sails.

For all these reasons, he thanked God for this job after three months of nothing. Yet, he was not completely comfortable with the idea of starting it. Somehow, he had a bad feeling about it.

After haggling ten thousand euros on the phone with the employer for the demolition of the building, the rubble cleaning and ground reclamation, Dragan was asked to go on site for an inspection on the following day.

When asking for the address, the owner – an elderly farmer – hung up without notice.

How weird was that? Dragan thought.

The young Romanian didn't know the little town of Aguscello, in the outskirts of Ferrara. He was living in the provincial capital and rarely would he go around for a walk in the open country.

While drinking his coffee at the Centre café, Dragan asked for information about how to get to Aguscello. The bartender's only answer was a kind of joke Dragan didn't get at first.

"What are you going to do over there? Do you want to visit somebody in the asylum? You are late, dude! It has been shut down for forty years by now." The barman said in an easy-going tone.

"Actually, I have to demolish a five-floor palace, but the employer forgot to tell me the address on the phone. I don't know exactly where it is."

"There's no such palace in Aguscello, my friend. I guess you mean the ex-asylum for children. A long time ago, it belonged to the Red Cross. They abandoned it back in the 70s... definitely not a nice story!"

Dragan felt suddenly uncomfortable at hearing those words.

For one second, he seriously thought of calling the farmer on the phone to reject the job offer. Not only for the lack of honesty on the old man's part – who had not mentioned the history of the building at all – but also because psychiatric Hospitals reminded him of the horror and desolation he had experienced in the orphanage in Romania where he had spent his entire childhood and his baby brother had died by meningitis.

Yet, what was he supposed to do?

He needed the money so bad. Eventually, Dragan didn't have the nerve to dial the farmer's number on his cell phone.

Still frozen in front of the giant gate, he pulled the sweater zip up to his throat; he squashed the smoking butt with the heel of his safety footwear and finally pushed the squeaking grating with the palm of his hand.

The walkway up to the building was dotted and covered with all sorts of weeds and ferns, so high in some spots that Dragan had to pull them out with his bare hands. A three-step flight led to the arch-shaped entrance. It looked roughly cemented. *Definitely a shoddy, rushed work,* he thought.

On the right, there was a breach in the wall at least five feet wide. Apparently, it was the only way through which one could sneak into the building. Once inside, Dragan found what must have been the Hospital courtyard: it was a devastated room, which was dotted with shards, pieces of fallen plaster and scattered debris all over; right in the middle, was rotting a little carousel for children, completely rusted and invaded by spider webs. The small seats were connected to a central coupling pin that, due to the passing of time and exposure to atmospheric agents, was slightly dangling on one side.

An asylum with a playroom?

Dragan felt a freezing shiver along his spine and a cold frisson all over his skin. He took a look around and noticed that the four walls, which were molded and scraped overall, seemed to be on the verge of falling down any moment. They were covered with a lot of murals and spray paintings. Dragan got closer to one of them, trying to decipher it, when a voice, come out of nowhere, made him jump.

"You must be the bricklayer."

"Hey! Yes, it's me, Iliescu. You must be the owner."

"If a roof tile falls down onto your head, do not expect me to compensate you! Forewarned is forearmed!" The old man said in a peremptory tone.

"Sorry, I just wanted to get a sense of the work I have to do." Dragan tried to apologize, well aware that he had left his protective helmet inside the van.

"Follow me. I'll show you what must be done." Was the farmer's only answer.

From the courtyard, they walked carefully close to the walls until they reached the big entrance hall of the ground floor. In the far corner, there was the only accessible stairwell in the entire building.

"The stairs go up to the second floor included; after that, you need to figure out something. They have collapsed, along with the ceiling. Be careful; put one foot after the other." The old man was already climbing up, putting his own feet on the first step.

Dragan had already noticed the bad condition of the stairs, as well as the rest of the building. This didn't surprise him, given the cheap material used to build all the buildings in Italy in the 1950s.

Stepping slowly, not knowing whether the precarious steps would carry his weight, he went ahead of the old man, who had stopped halfway; while climbing, he tore off some spider webs; got rid of a little rafter and a few other stumbling blocks, and eventually stopped on the first floor.

Even though sunlight was filtering from the broken shutters and the courtyard breach, Dragan couldn't see farther than his nose.

He tried to lay his right foot on a tile to test it, but he realized this could collapse under his weight anytime now. He couldn't take that chance.

"I need to go back to my van and recover my helmet". He said to the owner, still standing halfway. "I want to make sure I'll place the explosive charges at the bottom of the bearing walls. I can't see anything from here; I have to get closer."

The old man didn't reply. He took a step back towards the wall to let Dragan pass and opened his arms in a gesture of impatience.

"Make it quick!" He spat out angrily.

The young Romanian pretended not to notice the farmer's rudeness and climbed down the few steps to reach the ground floor again. He gained the breach in the wall, being careful at the sharp potsherd and pieces of glass scattered all over; he recovered the helmet from the van, tested the forehead light to see if it was working, and rushed again towards the building. As soon as he put his feet on the devastated pavement of the courtyard, Dragan felt a new cold wave grabbing his stomach, as if there was a temperature range between the outside and the inside. That was the third time he was feeling that cold, even though it was a beautiful late March day and the sun was already shining.

Out of the corner of his eye, he saw the carousel moving. This was weird. Sitting on one of the small seats, there was a child, ten years old or so. He was dressed up only in a white shirt and a pair of shorts of the same color. Dragan could swear that going to the van and coming back had only taken a couple of minutes at the most; he could also swear that the boy was not there two minutes earlier.

"Hey, what you're doing here?" He asked. He sounded a bit surprised, despite himself. "Aren't you cold? Do your parents know you come and play over here?"

"*Ring around the rosie...* Do you want to play with me?" The little boy asked without replying to Dragan's question, slightly tilting his head to the right.

"You can get hurt, you know that? Do you live somewhere near? Where is your mum?"

"*A pocket full of posies, ashes, ashes, we all fall down!*"

"Come here. Let's go call your parents before you..."

"Do you want to play, too? Ring around the rosie..." The child was still singing, impassively.

"I can't. I have to work. Come on! Get off the carousel. The ceiling could fall down anytime, see? Give me your hand. I'll walk you outside." Dragan was trying to talk him into doing the right thing for his own sake, offering his own hand to earn his trust.

"Why don't you adults let us play?"

"*Us*? Did you bring some friends with you? Where are they?"

"We play here all the time..." The boy replied while the carousel was still moving, squeaking on the coupling pin.

Dragan thought the baby boy could be suffering from autism. He had tried to attract his attention, but the child would not either answer questions or react to visual stimulation: when he had offered his hand to get him off the carousel, the child didn't even look at it. Dragan was worried about his safety, but he was also afraid of his possible reactions: if he had picked him up into his arms, would the boy start to scream? He didn't know how to handle a child, much less one having a disorder.

"Wait here. I'll go call the owner."

"Will you play with me a little while?"

"Yeah, I will be back in a minute. I promise."

Dragan walked again towards the entrance hall and found the farmer in the same spot, smoking a cigar and puffing out the smoke. He looked impatient and bored.

"There's a child in the courtyard. If he gets hurt, you will end up in a lot of troubles, you know that?"

"What the hell are you talking about? I've been standing right here since you left and nobody has sneaked in from the breach."

"I told you there's a boy in the courtyard! If you don't believe me, maybe you'll believe your eyes. Come and see. Be my guest! I'm telling you this because if something bad happens, the police will knock on your door, not mine!"

"I will kick his ass right away! Let me pass. Erodes was right: babies should all be killed..."

Dragan pretended not to hear that inappropriate joke and followed the old man up to the courtyard. He was determined to pick the boy up into his arms this time, no matter what, and to walk him outside for his own sake. He hoped that the child wouldn't get too nervous and wouldn't try to free himself because if he did, he would surely escape.

When they reached the courtyard, Dragan froze on the threshold. The little boy was gone.

"Are you nuts?" The farmer asked.

"I promise you there was a boy here until a minute ago, playing on the carousel. Where could he have got to? I didn't even ask him for his name... Hey, where are you?" The Romanian asked the void, raising his voice to be heard. He also took a look at the walkway from the breach in the wall, to see if the child had gone that way.

"Who cares!? Do not waste my time!" The owner shouted at him.

"Ok, ok, I'll finish the inspection and then I'll look for him by myself. I am sure he was standing there. I'm not crazy..."

Dragan adjusted the helmet on his head and made towards the staircase again. He couldn't help but think about the child. He couldn't help but regret his hesitation to grab him in the first place, and get him safe. He hoped so bad that the child wouldn't get hurt. He didn't want to take into account an even worse scenario. *Poor child*, he thought. *I couldn't live with myself if anything were to happen to him. Who knows? Maybe he hid himself somewhere in the building... I hope that he will be careful.*

Dragan easily climbed up to the first floor; walked a few steps along the bearing wall, taking advantage of the helmet light to locate the most resistant beams; eventually, he reached what once was a wide wing of the psychiatric Hospital. He noticed that a five-pointed star had been roughly drawn on the cobblestone. Right in the middle of it, he could clearly see the ashes of some makeshift fire and a few organic remains, too. He had no doubts: someone had performed a satanic ritual.

He stuck to the wall, paying attention to where he was putting his feet; then he reached the hinges of what once must have been a door and leaned slightly forward to take a peek. It was a little square room, which was completely empty except for a rusted box spring in the far corner.

A creepy shiver climbed up his spine to his very neck when Dragan recalled the bartender's words back at the coffee shop: electroshock was a usually performed procedure in this specific asylum, especially on unmanageable patients.

He shook his head and sighed, trying to dismiss his childhood memories from his mind, when he had lived in a Romanian orphanage along with his little brother. Despite his efforts to forget that part of his young life, he could still remember the atrocious screams coming from the top-floor. The access to that section of the orphanage was prohibited to every child if unaccompanied.

Dragan closed his eyes for a couple of seconds. When he heard something dart past him through the window, he re-opened them just in time to see a pigeon bash into the opposite wall. *Intentionally.*

What the hell...?

He pronounced these words aloud, but the last thing he expected to see was condensation before his mouth. He took a step back in astonishment.

It was 60 degrees when I got here. How is this even possible?

He turned, took the same path back and started climbing up to the second floor. On the last step, a swear word in Romanian slipped out of his lips: the ceiling had collapsed and dragged almost the entire floor down with it. Placing the explosive charges would take him a nearly six-feet-long jump, not to mention whether the beams would hold up the impact or would bear his weight, if he ever found a way to reach the third floor.

"I'm coming down; I am finished!" He shouted at the farmer, who was still waiting on the first floor.

"Won't you let us play anymore?" The same little boy from the carousel asked Dragan abruptly. It looked like he had come out of nowhere. He was sitting on a beam that was dangling in space, stuck between the stairs' handrail and the opposite bearing wall.

"Hey you! How did you end up here?" Dragan asked. He was happy to find him safe and sound but at the same time, was alarmed by the dangerous situation the baby boy had put himself into.

"Won't you play with us?"

"It's too risky, I already told you. Where did you leave your friends?"

"We just want to play a little bit..."

"Come over to me. I'll walk you home to your mum. Jesus, how can I do to pick you up safely?"

"Who are you fucking talking to? Are you coming down or what?" The old man asked Dragan. He sounded quite impatient as usual.

"The child I talked you about, has climbed up here. Damn it! I told you I was not nuts. He is sitting at least thirty feet from the ground! Do you have a ladder or something?"

"There's a stepladder in my barn, but it's not that long..."

"It will do the trick. I'll use it as a lever against the wall so I will be able to reach him. Hurry! The boy could fall down any moment now."

"Damned kids... They are the last fucking problem I need right now!" The old man was muttering, while making towards the breach in the wall.

"Stay there, ok?" – Dragan addressed the little boy again, trying hard to keep his voice tone calm – "How did you get to sit over there?"

"Why don't you play with us? *Ring around the rosie...*" The child was repeating the rhyme over and over, letting his legs dangling in space.

"No, no, no, don't move! Now, I'm going to pick you up so we can go and play outside, ok?"

"I want to play *NOW*."

"Yeah, yeah, we'll play together as soon as we get down. I promise."

72

Dragan walked a few steps on the remaining floor, but there was a twenty-feet-wide hole in front of him: to get to the beam where the boy was sitting, he needed something to bridge the gap. Even a rope or another beam, whatever it took.

How long will the owner take to come back? He thought, prey to frustration.

He leaned a bit forward, putting one foot on the precarious border of the flooring. Unfortunately, there were still six feet to go between the beam and his fingertips.

"Don't move; do you hear me? What's your name?"

"Are you here to play with us?"

"Yes, yes, I promise. I will play with you. Is there anyone else with you? You can tell me; don't be afraid. You could get hurt, you know?"

"*A pocket full of posies, ashes, ashes, we all fall DOWN!*"

As soon as the boy was finished singing the nursery rhyme, he threw himself into the void.

"Nooo!" Dragan shouted with all his voice. He brought his hands to his face and closed his eyes for a few seconds. Then he took a deep, long breath and looked into the thirty-foot-deep hole under his feet. His heart was beating into his very ears. Among the debris and the shards, he was not able to locate the body of the little boy; the light filtering from the outside was not enough to sight something clearly. Besides, light was creating weird reflections. Suddenly, Dragan came up with an idea: he took his helmet off his head and pointed the forehead light downwards. Still, there was no sign of the child.

"I said: we all fall *down*!" The boy said angrily. All of a sudden, he had appeared behind Dragan's shoulders.

The young Romanian felt a tiny, almost imperceptible electrical shock on his right hip. This made him lose his already precarious balance. Instinctively, he tried to grab himself onto something, but the beam was far too away from his reach.

He lost the grip of his left foot and fell down into the void. A second later, the freezing sensation he had been intermittently feeling throughout the morning, wrapped him in a kind of cocoon, immobilizing him. In the impact against the trash and the stones thirty feet further down, his neck got broken on the instant.

The little boy, who was still standing on the second floor, took a step forward and picked the helmet up, enjoying himself, casting its light upon the walls.

Slightly bending his head on his right shoulder, he morbidly watched five children, popped out of nowhere, as they grabbed the bricklayer's body by his feet and carried him deep down into the basement. They were singing the same nursery rhyme in unison. They vanished into the building bowels, as suddenly as they had appeared. When the boy overheard the typical crawling steps and troubling breathing of the old farmer, he disappeared in a flash, too, letting go of his grip on the helmet, which slowly rolled towards the hole. In the impact against the ground, the forehead light broke into a dozen pieces.

"Here I am! I've got only this one..." The old man said aloud, after laying the stepladder on the nearest wall, in order to catch his breath. He raised his eyes and tried to focus on the point where he remembered the bricklayer was standing before he left to recover the ladder.

"Hey, are you there? Do you hear me? Damn it; I don't even know his name... Hey Romania, where are you?" He asked the void, with his nose up in the air.

There was no answer.

"Fuck off! Don't tell me this one has stood me up too! No way! It's a bloody curse! I can't find anyone to demolish this wreck of a building!" He muttered in frustration. He made towards the breach in the courtyard, to see if the bricklayer had returned to his van to recover whatever he might need. Sticking to the wall, he saw that the carousel in the room was moving by itself. Yet, there were no draft or airflow. The old man stood on the threshold for one moment, until his eyes focused on a spray-made writing upon the plaster.

Whoever makes the carousel spin won't be able to stop it anymore, since the children's souls will play forever and a day.

The last time he had checked the room two weeks before, this puzzling writing was definitely not there.

The farmer crossed over the breach in the wall and took a look at the street: the van was still parked in the same place, but there was no sign of the bricklayer. He looked again at the wrecked Hospital and shook his head.

"Damned children..." He blurted out, walking back home with a resigned look on his face.

Occam's razor

1. *The motive*

"We were sitting around a bonfire... all the four of us".

Brian Atwood was speaking from the witness box during the first hearing of the trial.

"We'd been hanging around on Santa Monica Beach for a while when we came up with the idea of lighting a bonfire. Far away from the pier, of course; the last thing we wanted was to be caught in the act by the police. Zachary and I wanted to create some romantic atmosphere so that Christine and Taylor would have sex with us in the end. We thought "why not? We light a bonfire, we drink a few beers and after that, maybe...". We had picked the girls up at the pier party earlier that night, but they were being difficult, I mean bitchy, you know? They would turn us down if we tried to kiss or hug them. Once the fire was up, we found ourselves short of stuff to talk about. We're definitely not the kind of guys who like talking, you know? So, when the situation was about to turn awkward, Christine suggested some sort of a game: "Each and every one of us must confess his / her darkest secret; even something we are ashamed of or we never had the nerve to tell anybody. After that, we vote for the most ridiculous, awkward secret. The second round of beer is on the one who loses. Are you in?"

We all said yes, since it was crystal clear that the girls were not willing to get to the point, if you know what I mean. What else could we do? Christine confessed she had passed the driving test thanks to a huge help from the instructor. Taylor confessed she had stolen a top in some Versace shop in Sunset Boulevard. Eventually, was Zachary's turn to speak: "Five years ago, as I was reaching Tijuana, Mexico, to get some good, cheap cocaine, I ran over a girl with my car. She was jogging, poor bitch, and yes, I wasn't paying attention. Cigarettes had fallen under the passenger seat. It all happened so fast, damn it! I got away; I was fucking scared. I don't even know if she is still alive or she died instantly..."

At these words, Zach burst out laughing, and kept gulping down his beer. The three of us froze, all stunned. We got speechless. That was supposed to be a game; this was what Christine had in mind in the first place. We really could not imagine it would turn into a nightmare. We could not expect such a confession to be made.

"Are you kidding me?" – Christine was the first to break the silence – "You didn't even call 911?"

"There's no such thing in Mexico. I was scared and I ran away, ok? What was I supposed to do?"

Zachary was clearly drunk. Most likely, he did not even realize the consequences his words were implying. He spoke again in an ironic tone: "The impact of the crash dented the bonnet, so I also had to pay damages to the car rental."

"You're a fucking murderer!" Christine shouted in his face, in full disgust. She got to her feet and took leave from the beach.

"Where the hell are you going?"

"To tell the police! You just confessed a murder in front of three people."

"What? I was joking! Come back here!" Zachary's excuse was that he was trying to impress the girls with this story. He stood up and ran after

Christine. "Hey, I was making it all up! I was just trying to be a hit with you guys... Damn it, stop!"

He reached her and grabbed her arm. Christine struggled to get free and yelled to get his hands off of her. Taylor rushed to her aid and ordered Zachary to keep away from them: "Don't you dare follow us!" She shouted in a threatening voice. I stood up, too, and ran up to them. I stopped Zach with my body. He looked like he was not willing to give up. He kept begging them not to report him to the police for something he had clearly made up, for something he was not really responsible for. I took him to the parking space where he had left his bike, about a mile away from the beach. Disappearing was the most sensible thing to do after screwing up the party like that. I did not even ask him if the story was true or not. It just sounded ridiculous. I just thought he was under the influence of alcohol. After that, I went back home. I haven't seen Zachary since we said good night at the parking space. The following day, I recognized Christine's picture on TV, at 1.00 p.m. Breaking News: they were announcing she was found dead in her house in Pasadena at 9.00 a.m., with clear signs of choking on her neck. I called Zachary on the phone, but his cell was off. They had already taken him into custody, on a charge of second-degree murder. They easily reached out to him, given his criminal record and the history of drug deal, as soon as Taylor mentioned his name.

2. *The Defense*

Jonathan Riley, the defense, was walking back and forth in the enormous courtroom of East Los Angeles Courthouse. His arms were folded. He was waiting for the witness to bring his speech to an end. After listening to his version of what happened that tragic night, Riley unfastened the first button of his jacket and put both his hands in the suit pockets. Eventually, he asked: "Mr. Atwood, do you know Miss Christine Remington's address?"

"On the News, they said she lived in a small apartment in Pasadena, near the Tennis Club. Sorry, I can't remember the address exactly." Brian replied, changing position on the witness chair. He did not look at ease with his sworn testimony.

"You may also know that the coroner determined the time of death accurately enough, between 2.30 a.m. and 3.00 a.m. that same night." Riley made sure to underline the importance of this lapse of time.

"Yeah, I read the papers..." The young man nodded in response.

"Mr. Atwood, please tell us what time it was when you saw Christine run away furiously from the bonfire place on Santa Monica Beach."

"Just before 01.30 a.m."

"So, let us say that at about 1.25 a.m., you saw the victim going back to the pier party. We know that her friend, Miss Taylor Adler, the last person to see Christine alive if we don't take the murderer into account, drove her home to Pasadena at 2.10 a.m. / 2.15 a.m. at the latest. Miss Adler claims she persuaded Miss Remington not to press charges on the defendant, Zachary Quilmes. Eventually, she talked her into letting go of the whole matter. One hour after that, at the latest, the coroner says Christine was already dead. Now, I'm asking you, Mr. Atwood: my client, Mr. Quilmes, could have followed the two girls on his bike, driving completely unnoticed? Could have he waited for Miss Adler to be gone and then have sneaked in the apartment to suffocate Christine?"

Brian Atwood did not reply. He lowered his eyes as if he was trying to gain time.

"Do I need to remind you that you are under oath, Mr. Atw...?"

"Yes, it's a likely scenario." Brian admitted despite himself and his ten-year friendship with Zachary Quilmes.

"Do you agree with Prosecution when they claim Mr. Quilmes was afraid that Miss Remington could report him to the police?"

"He looked worried about that, yes."

"What if I told you that at 2.52 a.m. of that very night, Mr. Quilmes was standing in front of an automatic machine twenty-five miles away from the murder place?" Jonathan Riley announced triumphantly, turning on a LCD TV in the middle of the courtroom. "Your Honor, the defense demands to put on record the security video from the vending machine located at 1249 Bel Air Road. My client can be clearly seen as he stands in front of it for at least five minutes, intent on getting something to drink." Riley kept speaking in a solemn voice tone, while the irrefutable footage was displayed on the monitor, showing Quilmes messing with the drink dispenser. "Mr. Atwood, is it possible to be in Pasadena at 2.30 a.m., busy killing a poor innocent girl, and also be in Bel Air twenty minutes later, twenty-five miles away, busy drinking beer in complete relaxation? I am not a mathematician, but my consultants assure me that the defendant should have flown, *literally* flown, speeding at 130 miles per hour, without ever braking or stopping at the traffic lights or slowing down on a bend. Let us take for granted that if you have just killed someone, you don't choose the highway. We all agree on this, right? Don't you find a little weird that Christine let my client in her home? He was the guy she had just had an argument with two hours earlier; she deemed him a murderer, a hit-and-run driver! How could she have let him in? Yet, Forensics has assured that there are no signs of breaking on doors or windows; therefore, the victim must have opened the door and let her assaulter in. Weird, huh? No trace of Quilmes' DNA was found in Pasadena apartment. I'm not taking into consideration the DNA that was found on the victim, since my client had wooed Miss Remington, touched and hugged her two hours before she died. So, I'm asking you, Mr. Atwood –and I beg you to answer directly to the ladies and gentlemen of the jury – in your opinion, my client can physically be Miss Remington's killer?"

"If in that specific lapse of time he was in Bel Air, no, he cannot be the man. He can't have killed Christine." Brian said, addressing the juries.

"Your Honor, I demand for the Bel Air video to be officially put on record as evidence, so that my Prosecution colleagues will be allowed to watch it and verify its reliability. I have no further questions." Jonathan Riley concluded. He looked quite satisfied in his double-breasted suit.

3. *The Prosecution*

The assistant district attorney, Anthony De Vito, stood up and cleared his throat. He asked the judge for the permission to approach his bench and asked him to grant an adjournment. That video, coming out from nowhere, had made Prosecution "framework" fall down like a house of cards. De Vito needed time to get his ideas straight.

One thing he knew for sure was that Zachary Quilmes had the motive – namely, the raging impulse to shut the mouth of the person who could send him to jail for a lifetime – but apparently, he also had a strong alibi. De Vito already knew that his staff would not find any inconsistency in the footage the defense had just provided. He did not expect to find some sort of loop sequences or superimposed images on the video. He had known Jonathan Riley since college times, so he was perfectly aware that this was his personal masterpiece, one that he had kept for the very last moment. It was an ace up his sleeve.

Taking advantage of the adjournment, De Vito entered a room equipped with all the necessary pieces of technology. The L.A. Courthouse would put it at lawyers' disposal in case of need. And De Vito *really* needed to watch that video.

The man that at 2.52 a.m. was pulling off a beer from the automatic dispenser in Bel Air road was definitely the defendant, no doubt about it. So, who the hell could have killed the girl? Anthony De Vito needed to make up a new Prosecution strategy in less than forty-five minutes.

Yet, he could not easily embrace a scenario in which Quilmes was innocent. In his opinion, this was a crystal clear case in the first place. It was going to be an easy victory, a smooth success in court. Well, honestly, until a few minutes ago. Now, that video was screwing it all up.

Christine Remington did not have enemies or jealous ex-fiancés. So what? No, Anthony De Vito was positive: Zachary Quilmes was *still* his man.

What the hell?! Nobody has the gift of ubiquity! Unless...

"Your Honor, the Prosecution calls on Zachary Alejandro Quilmes to give evidence." De Vito announced in a strong voice when the hearing resumed.

The young man, dressed in a linen suit that looked too tight for his muscular body, stood up and made towards the witness chair, without betraying any emotion on his face. His blond hair was full of cheap, poor-quality gel and an uncultivated beard was the heritage of the days he had already spent in jail.

"Mr. Quilmes, did you kill Miss Remington?"

"Objection, Your Honor! This is unacceptable!" The defense Riley protested immediately, jumping on his chair.

"Ok, ok, sorry! I'll take that back..." De Vito said, making an apology gesture by raising both his palms. "I'll try my best to formulate my question another way: who did you get to kill her in your place?"

"Objection!" His colleague shouted again; his face had turned almost red due to his growing indignation.

"Prosecutor, this is the first and last warning. After that, I will charge you with contempt of court. Are we clear?" Judge Thompson declared, glowering at De Vito from head to toe.

"I sincerely apologize, Your Honor; it won't happen again" – the assistant district attorney defended himself and continued: "Please allow me a few questions. Mr. Quilmes, how come were you hanging around in Bel Air residential area so late at night? I know you live in Muscle Beach, am I correct? Please do not tell me that for a couple of beers you were willing to drive for twelve miles! But... wait a minute: Santa Monica's parking place, where you left your bike, is not even on the way to Bel Air! Can you explain that?"

"How can I possibly remember that? More than three months have elapsed..." – Zachary replied, shrugging his shoulders – "Maybe there was another party in Bel Air or most likely, I picked up some girl in the neighborhood." He concluded in an insolent tone, arching his eyebrows for effect.

"Hmm... these girls, Mr. Quilmes, they seem to have the power to drive you crazy, huh?"

"What is that supposed to mean?"

"Oh, let us see... October 2001: charge of sexual harassment brought by a female UCLA student. Does this ring any bells?"

"I was found not guilty. She had made everything up."

"Hmm... sounds interesting... What about this? March 2003: charge of violence and abuse brought by Maureen Sheldon, your girlfriend at the time. Was she telling lies, too?"

"She would scratch me on my face and my back, so I just fought back. That's it..." Quilmes replied with arrogance. He was sitting on the chair in complete relaxation, as if he was at the movies instead of a courtroom.

"Objection!" Jonathan Riley jumped to his feet and protested again. "What has this got to do with the case? That's irrelevant!"

"Granted!" – The Judge shouted – "Attorney, I already warned you. Get to the point!"

"I am going to, Your Honor. Mr. Quilmes, how did you feel for the victim? Did you love her? Were you fond of her?"

"I felt nothing; I just wanted to have sex with her."

"You felt nothing... right. So, I guess you were not sorry at all at hearing that a poor 22-year girl died, were you?"

"I didn't say that."

"I also guess that you were not sorry at the time of the accident in Mexico, when you ran over a jogger and you left her in the throes of death on the street, huh?"

"This never happened! I made it up just to impress the girls..."

"You didn't call for medical assistance or an ambulance, Mr. Quilmes, because if the girl had survived, you would be rotting in jail right now. If she had gotten the chance to talk and tell what happened, you would not be able to enjoy your life, your money, your freedom and easy sex now! That woman was a threat to you, just the way Christine Remington was: that's why *she had to die*. Most likely, she was not going to be reasonable; she was a young woman who believed in justice and had moral principles that pushed her to do the right thing. All this would have an unpleasant consequence for you: you would have lost your freedom, your lifestyle and your reputation. Am I wrong, Mr. Quilmes? You like that sense of power upon women, don't you, *Zachary*? I wonder what kind of relationship you had with your mother when you were a child... I tried to reach her on the phone, to ask her to come here and give evidence, but she answered that she is scared... Sorry, I really need to quote her here: "*He scares the crap out of me*". Oh, maybe this one finally has to do with our case: "911 call coming from Eloisia Quilmes, August 1999. She is showing bruises, scratches and hematomas...""

"Screw you, asshole! I'm going to kill you!" Zachary Quilmes shouted. He looked out of his mind; he jumped over the witness box and hurled himself at De Vito. The security guard who was on duty in the courtroom that morning, intervened promptly and blocked Quilmes, grabbing his hands and holding them tight behind his back.

Upon the judge's decision, the defendant was handcuffed and escorted to the prison cell behind the courtroom. He kept insulting the attorney all along.

"Silence in court or I will clear the room!" Thompson was trying to keep the situation under control.

Anthony De Vito was smiling mischievously when he reached his chair again. He had achieved his purpose: he had sown the seed of doubt in each and every jury's mind.

4. *The sentence*

Both the attorneys addressed the court before the sentence was carried out. Each summary took about forty minutes. On the one hand, Riley insisted on the weakness of every circumstantial evidence and on the reasonable doubt that his client could have committed the murder in such a narrow lapse of time; on the other hand, De Vito stressed the clear, serious problem the defendant was suffering from – anger management – and also insisted on the fact that Christine Remington did not have enemies at all, nor any stalking ex-boyfriends.

Five days later, both their cell phones rang at the same time.

"The defendant rise, please. Mr. Spokesman, did you reach a verdict?" Judge Thompson asked the man who was sitting in the first line of the jury.

"Yes, Your Honor" – he replied, standing – "We find the defendant, Zachary Quilmes... not guilty of second-degree murder."

The assistant district attorney Anthony De Vito closed his eyes, holding his breath for a few seconds. At hearing such a ridiculous sentence, he swallowed twice, feeling his Adam's apple heavy like a stone. Then he roused, picked up all his papers and documents into his briefcase, and made towards the exit without telling a word to his staff or exchanging looks with them or shaking their hands. All along his eleven-year career, he had always brought the guilty to justice and this was the very first time he failed. Deep down his heart, Anthony De Vito knew that Zachary Quilmes was the killer. His guts were not failing him. They never had. His sixth sense was pushing in the same direction.

"Attorney?"

He heard someone call out to him as he was waiting for his limo, standing on the last steps of the Courthouse. De Vito turned back. He was stunned at realizing that voice was coming from somebody who still had the nerve to address him. "Blessed be technology, huh?" – Quilmes was being ironical while approaching – "If it wasn't for that camera, I would have ended up in jail... *Unfairly*. You thought you were going to win, didn't you? You got very close, I must admit that! Frankly, I walked on the sharp edge of a sword. No, not actually a sword, rather a *razor*... oh yeah, an *Occam's razor*!" He concluded for effect, winking at De Vito. That said, he pointed at the journalists who were already waiting for him.

The assistant district attorney froze on the spot, still gazing at him. What the hell was that supposed to mean? And what about the winking?

Let me get this straight: did he actually say Occam's razor? Oh yes, sure, he thought, recalling the methodological principle he had once read in some college book: among several possible solutions, it is reasonable to choose the simplest and most plausible one. Further possibilities are useless if the first one is enough and fitting.

Zachary Quilmes had just handed a message to him. That was his last affront. A little sweetener for the attorney who had just lost; a beanie that confirmed De Vito was right despite the defeat. Yes, Zachary Quilmes was guilty. *He had just winked at the Prosecutor to let him know!* If he was not the executioner, he was at least the instigator. No doubt about it.

Yes, Anthony de Vito's instincts did not fail him, not even in that case.

Three days later

In his office, on the top floor in the highest skyscraper of Los Angeles, the assistant district attorney was filing papers and documents regarding the Quilmes case. While clearing his desk from useless sheets, he happened to find a CD-ROM under a pile of reams. A yellow Post-it was roughly stuck on it; apparently, the handwriting belonged to his personal secretary. The message said: "Security video Bel Air Road, 200% zoom".

Anthony De Vito could not say how long that CD had been lying unnoticed on his desk, hidden amidst all papers and stuff. He opened the plastic holder, pulled the CD out and inserted it into the specific tray of his personal laptop. After that, he just waited for the player to buffer. A few seconds later, the attorney was watching Zachary Quilmes arrive in front of the automatic machine, on May 19 at 2.52 a.m., as it was clearly superimposed on the monitor in the right low corner. De Vito could perfectly see the young man insert the coins, raise his eyes towards the camera and finally grab the beer from the dispenser.

While waiting, Quilmes was moving his neck from side to side, maybe to do some stretching. Eventually, he disappeared from the camera angle.

De Vito sat tight on the chair and pushed the rewind command on the player: he had noticed something weird. He just wanted to make sure of it. He pushed the "stop" button the very instant Quilmes was stretching his neck on the right shoulder; the attorney checked the "wide screen" box on the monitor and suddenly, he saw it.

From under the huge collar of Quilmes' t-shirt, a sun-like tattoo was popping up. It was drawn on the shoulder blade muscle. De Vito felt dazed and bewildered; a pair of pulsing veins were showing up on his sweating forehead. A tiny little doubt started making its road through his mind.

He stood up and began searching furiously in his briefcase, among the documents and papers, and in the desk drawers, too: he was sure he had stored somewhere the mug shots of Quilmes taken on the morning he was arrested, a few hours after the murder. Quilmes was asked to turn sideways so that one of the pictures could be taken in profile.

"Here you are!" De Vito exclaimed, prey to adrenaline. His own voice in all that silence made him jump. The room was completely soundproofed.

Zachary Quilmes was taken into custody while in his night pants and shirt. His neck looked well-tanned; it was fully visible and exposed, without any drawing, design, stain, bruise or birthmark. A tattoo could not have disappeared out of magic between 2.52 a.m. and 11.00 a.m. of the same morning.

Anthony De Vito jumped on the chair. He kept staring at an indefinite point in front of him. His arms were dangling along his hips. The mug shot of Quilmes slipped away from his fingers onto the floor and slowly landed on the parquet.

The Occam's razor: the solution is often the simplest one.

Nobody can be everywhere at the same time.

Zachary Quilmes had *a twin brother*.

A cast-iron alibi.

19th May 2010,
2.41 a.m.

"Hello?"

"Xander, can you hear me? This is Zach. I screwed up... I need your help!"

"Zach? You dumb ass! What the fuck do you want? I told you to call me only when the "stuff" is on its way."

"No, no, it's not about that. I need your help, bro; I did a hell of a mess this time. A fucking bitch wouldn't stop crying so I squeezed her neck a little too much... Jesus, I didn't want to hurt her; I just wanted to frighten her!"

"What are you talking about? You killed *una chica*?"

"Yeah, I did. It was not my fault, I swear! That was not my intention in the first place. I don't want to spend the rest of my life in jail, Xander; I need your help, please!"

"Where are you calling me from? Tell me you're not using your cell!"

"No, no, I just got away from Pasadena and I stopped by a pay phone on the street... You owe me one, bro, remember? I saved your ass when you killed that girl in Tijuana five years ago. I helped you in with the green card..."

"What the fuck do you want me to do?" Xander interrupted his brother abruptly.

"You need to go out and make sure that people will see you, in a crowded bar, for example, or a party, whatever! Make something showy or flashy, something that won't pass unnoticed. People must remember you were there at this exact time. You need to do this right now, man, otherwise timing won't match. Hurry! You could also make a rude gesture at an intersection camera, or at a service station... Everything will do the trick! Just make sure your face will be clearly visible, ok? Hurry, Xander! I've got a countdown going on here..."

"After that, we are even. Are we clear? I'll save your ass this time so I won't owe you anything more. Got it?"

"Yeah, yeah, bro, sure!"

"I'll drop by to buy some beers. I've just finished them. When the police takes you into custody, they will question you: tell them you were standing at the self-service dispenser in Bel Air Road. It will take me ten minutes to get there."

"Great, perfect! You're a genius, bro!"

"Fuck you, idiot! Do not call me ever again."

Xander Quilmes – Wayne Finley for US Central Residential Register – interrupted the phone call abruptly, pushing the red button on the keyboard of the disposable cell phone he had just bought a week before. He dressed up, wearing a simple t-shirt; he grabbed a few coins from the shelf in the hall and got out of the house. He made towards the automatic machine three blocks away. He looked perfectly at ease; he pulled the battery off of the phone, crashed it twice with the heel of his shoe and let it drop into a manhole.

You owe me two bucks, bro, of unused credit... he thought, fastening his pace.

5. *Epilogue*

After the case was re-opened, only two months later was US coast guard able to locate Zachary Quilmes on board his yacht, miles away from the Miami harbor. Arresting him was not possible since FBI has no jurisdiction in international waters. Quilmes is being constantly watched. Police hopes he will make a mistake or a wrong turn that could bring him back within two hundred nautical miles. Until nowadays, he is still traveling around seas completely free, on board his boat.

On the contrary, Xander Quilmes/Wayne Finley's position remains unknown.

The House is in charge

"We've got to take action before it's too late."

"Yeah, I agree. It's just... what are we supposed to do?"

Marker turned in place and drew a small question mark among the scrabbles that Linda would usually make on the papers, sheets and notes she left beside the telephone.

Pencil looked at Marker. It sounded inconsolable when it said: "Let's try to leave her a message."

"No, she could grow suspicious and think there is a ghost here in Da House. She could run away in terror, leaving all of us behind. You know I love Linda and I would never do anything in the world that could frighten her. Add the conditions she's been living in in the last months."

Pencil slowly shook its tip towards the woman who was entering the room at that moment. The two objects did not move an inch. They froze on the desk, quietly observing the fast movements Linda's big hands were making. Suddenly, Marker felt it was being grabbed. It held its breath and closed its eyes. It was raised up high in the air, about to be thrown far away.

Linda never behaved badly like that. At least, not until that day. Marker was thrown against Russian Doll, which was caught unawares and fell from the shelf; it spilled open onto the floor and let drop a couple of its daughters, which were still asleep.

"*Chisda mati!*"

Russian Doll furiously tried to crawl to its daughters in order to calm them down. In the crash, one of them had lost a tiny stain of color on its forehead and was about to burst out into tears. Luckily, it was able to keep silent. Its mom began caressing it fondly by slightly swinging.

Marker had sneaked under the bed to prevent Linda from throwing it too. In the meantime, the girl went out of Da House. The door slammed behind her. On the room, descended a stunned, unusual silence.

***

A month had passed by since this episode. Linda's temper had been getting worse in an alarming way.

Pencil had been bitten and tossed into trash. It was rescued by its desk friends, which, all together, made Wastebasket fall on the floor. Eventually, they managed to pull Pencil out of it. As a precaution, they hid it behind the wardrobe.

The saddest fate was in store for Mug and Dish: they were broken the one against the other, while Frame was destroyed under Linda's feet and Picture of Mario (the husband Linda had left six months earlier) was torn apart into thousand pieces.

Other objects had gone through all sort of violence: Bedside Rug was being nervously kicked every single morning; Mario's Jacket, which had been forgotten by Mario in the closet, was torn apart into pieces by Linda by using Poultry Scissors; Block Notes was systematically tortured with deep and painful incisions, made by using Ballpoint Pen; not to mention Toby Teddy Bear, which, after being repeatedly thrown against the wall, had gone through some rips and had started losing stuffing from one of its shoulders and its butt.

House's patience lasted until the umpteenth, cruel murder three months later: Pincushion had its head torn off by Linda's nails. After that, all the objects made a joint decision: it was time to solve the problem once and for all. The date of their official meeting was settled on Tuesday, February 25, at 3.30 a.m. The better place to meet and talk unnoticed would be the study.

From the bathroom, would be arriving Toothbrush along with its Toothpaste. The kitchen would send Napkin and Fork, while Alarm Clock and Pillow, unable to take part in the meeting for obvious reasons, would delegate the twin Shoelaces and Cellular. From the patio, would be asked to attend the meeting Clothes Pin and its cousin Mop.

***

"Come on, guys... ssshhh... take it easy; keep quiet or you will wake her up!"

Shoelaces were snaking along the dark hall, gathering their companions together.

The objects that were asked to attend the meeting started walking towards the study; they had been tidily divided into groups and now, they were being careful at passing onto the tapestry, in order to smoothen every noise their movements would make.

The small "army" stopped in front of the study's door. Unexpectedly, they found it closed.

"Oh God! It's closed! Key must have forgotten about the meeting; most likely, it is still asleep."

Cellular turned to its companions. It looked worried.

"We have to go up to the keyhole and wake Key up."

"We got this!" The twin Shoelaces said. They jumped onto the jamb and began climbing twistingly towards the Key.

"Key!? Wake up! Come on, sleepyhead, wake up!" They whispered in its ear. They still were suffering from shortness of breath due to the climbing.

"What is it? Is this the appropriate time to come break my b*#@... Oops, sorry! I forgot about this!"

Clack! The door opened and all the objects walked in almost quietly until they reached the desk, where Pen, Paper Cutter and Pencil, which looked still bitten but at least restored to life, were impatiently waiting.

Lamp – everybody used to confidentially call her Firefly –turned on and addressed a pale ray of light upon the small group of friends.

"Thank you everybody, fella! This extraordinary meeting has been called so that we could discuss a highest priority situation. I guess you all know what I'm talking about."

Pencil took a good look around: everyone was nodding in response.

At that point, Cellular spoke to cut to the chase.

"I heard over the last phone call between Linda and his doctor. He sounded quite worried. Her violent reactions may be related to a still powerful feeling of anger towards Mario. She blames him for their marriage failure as well as her drawing career disappointment. The pain she's been suffering since they broke up, made her lose her job, her nearest and dearest, everything! She is alone now; she feels damaged and broken; as a result, she destroys all the things she has around, in compensation: namely... *us*."

"Let's kill her!" Paper Cutter suggested.

"Oh God, no! Pencil and I love Linda very much! We have already forgiven her. She is in a terrible condition; we have to help her out!" Marker could not believe that such a proposal had actually been made.

"Look how she reduced my Toothpaste!" Toothbrush replied acidly. Toothpaste was on its right side, barely standing and hardly trying to smile. Its body was marked by Linda's teeth prints and was showing the repeated twists it had been going through due to her angry outbursts. These last ones had caused serious injuries, until some blue menthol paste had begun popping out. "She won't stop, I bet! I agree with Cutter: let's kill her off!". Toothbrush was talking nonsense. Toothpaste looked at its friend with a resigned look on its face; eventually, it nodded in agreement, despite itself.

"Well, dear, why don't we give her one last chance? In fact, Linda's condition is hard and... we must admit that her behavior is not intentional." Pen was trying to address conversation towards a less drastic tone.

"It's right." – Clothes Pin said – "We have to help her. We must do that; it's our moral duty. Basically, we are the only friends she has left, after her total closure to the outside world. On the other hand, I don't understand how all this could have possibly happened." It concluded sadly.

"She was a girl so sweet and caring and pretty and nice..." Mop sighed, curling its completely torn strings.

"That's enough! I say, let's kill her. If we don't do that, sooner or later she will kill *us*. She will sweep us away one after the other. Have you already forgotten about Pincushion? What about Toby? It can't even crawl due to all the padding he's been losing. It was *her dear* Toby! They were inseparable. It has been her teddy bear since she was a child. Now what? Did you see how many punches she's been giving it lately? This afternoon, she has torn off one of its eyes! Here it is, take a look!"

One of the two Shoelaces that had just talked showed a small, black and bright button to all the group. Everybody took a step back. Their faces looked horrified.

"We have recovered it from under the tapestry. We can't go on like this. This must stop once and for all."

"I agree with Shoelaces and Cutter. So be it!" Toothbrush repeated, followed by its speechless companion.

Napkin and Fork kept silent. Debate was far from being over.

Suddenly, the door swung open. The chandelier was switched on in an instant, projecting all its light upon the small group of united objects at the bottom of the desk. They all froze on the spot. Lamp got prey to an unstoppable trembling.

Linda was there upon all of them, unbelieving and even angrier than usual.

"Damn you all!" She shouted, kicking the objects that were closer to her feet.

Mop and Fork flew off in the air. Then the girl grabbed Fork with her right hand: "How is it possible to find you here? And what about these ones?". Another big kick was given to Toothbrush; after that, she grabbed Paper Cutter and began tearing Napkin apart with an incredible vehemence.

Toothpaste fell down next to her Slipper. Linda took one second to crash it with all her might, jumping over it several times. Toothpaste blew out miserably, shooting its content onto the tapestry.

After this explosion of violence, which lasted a few minutes, the girl stopped, feeling exhausted and short of breath, and smiled. She had pulled out all the anger she had felt at the sight of all those things that were haphazardly gathered in her study.

"I'm nuts..." – she said to herself laughing out loud – "Maybe it's time I keep this wreck of a house a little more cleaned up."

Yawning rudely, she left the room, turning the switch off with a slap.

The objects were still scattered all over; some of them had landed onto the floor, someone else on the Table. Toothpaste, dead by now, was lying among its own bluish guts. Poor Toothbrush looked desperate. Pieces of Napkin were everywhere, also on the highest library shelves.

"Let's get rid of her." Cutter was growling. All of a sudden, it stood upright and slammed a hit with its blade on the floor.

"Yeah, let's do it! Tell us what we have to do."
Some of the rebellious ones replied in unison.
Pencil and Marker agreed despite themselves,
hoping that somehow, they would be able to avoid
the tragedy.

***

"Did you hear what they said? They're going to
kill her tonight!"

Pencil was moving back and forth, nervously
rolling upon the desk from one side to the other.

"Da House has made up its mind." Marker
answered sadly.

"What is that supposed to mean? This is not the
solution! We didn't really want to find one! These
are the solutions humans apply, not *us*! We are
behaving just like them. This is not like us. Instead
of helping her out, we have decided to kill her. Do
you realize the gravity of what I'm saying? This is
not like us; this is not our nature. We are meant
and supposed to help her. We've been created for
that. To help! I won't be part of this. I quit."

"Da house is in charge, my dear Pencil. It's in
charge."

Marker slowly got closer to Pencil and touched it
to calm it down.

"Who knows? Maybe at the very last moment, someone of the angriest ones will step back, so nothing bad will happen. I'm sorry to admit that I must adapt to our community decisions. What else could we do?"

"Yeah. What else can we do?"

The plan was arranged in the least details.

It would look like a suicide. Shoelaces, Fork and Cutter were appointed official executioners.

At an agreed signal, Shoelaces would be tying each other in order to make Linda fall down onto the floor; Fork would be jumping on her face to stab her in one of her eyes, and Cutter would be the one to finish her, cutting her throat clean off.

Pencil nervously scribbled off all afternoon long, thinking about a possible alternative over and over. Eventually, it came up with the idea of writing a message on a sheet so that Linda could read what was in store for her. Would she believe her eyes? Would she think of some ghost or some kind of creepy joke?

She would probably toss the note into trash without even stopping to read what was written on it. In the last few weeks, she had been living – rather, surviving – in complete neglect. She would pretend not to be home by not answering the phone; she would try her best to avoid visitors, especially her relatives or friends. Many of them had given up on going visit her. Every time they would stop by, she would start crying, yelling or talking nonsense. Every attempt to distract her or even make her smile turned out to be helpless or ended up frustrated.

Her ex-boyfriend Diego tried one time, bringing along a small, thin black diary.

"Look, Linda" – he told her in his funny way of speaking – "I found this in some pay phone a few days ago. On the inside, you can find the number of any priest or exorcist: there is also Father Amorth's one! What do you think? Shall I call him?"

The girl's only answer was to throw him out of Da House, pushing and kicking him in the ass.

"We're doing her a favor." Shoelaces murmured once they were ready to attack. Cutter and Fork had already been in place for a while. They were carefully holding position on the table.

Linda took a look at the clock and stood up. She was swinging a little when she tried to light a cigarette. Shoelaces tied each other to make her stumble. In no time, she fell down on the floor. Fork launched itself from the table but, instead of hitting Linda, it got stuck onto the tapestry and stood upright, vibrating.

In the attempt of holding onto something, Linda grabbed the cover of the sofa; Teddy Bear Toby, which was lying over there, fell down upon her face.

That was the moment when her psychological cork was suddenly uncapped.

She burst out into tears. Toby was staring at her with the only eye it had left. A bunch of wool was still popping out from its other eyehole.

"Forgive me, Toby. All of you guys, please forgive me. Please help me, please..." Linda was still lying on the floor, with Toby on her face, incapable of standing up. "I am tired; I am sick, sick of all this! Please help me! You guys help me out..."

Toby slowly slipped on one side and leaned against her shoulder, in order to defend her throat with its big head.

From the upside, Cutter, which was still on the table following the scene, took a step back and disappeared.

Cellular dialed the number of Linda's mother. In the meantime, every one of them drew close to their girl, waiting.

On a sunny day

"Silvius, come on! Let's play soccer! Who scores more penalties wins! You first; play the goalkeeper!"

"No, stop! My balloon is tired."

"What? Tired? It's not a living thing, come on! Hurry!"

"I said no! It is tired. End of discussion."

Chin up high, proud gaze, firm voice tone: he was not joking at all. Actually, I was the first one to lower my eyes in embarrassment.

"Ok, I'm going home. See you tomorrow!"

"No, wait! We can play hide and seek as the balloon rests. Start counting aloud, so I can hide myself. Don't peek!"

"One, two, three, four..."

I counted to thirty, then I opened my eyes and took a look around. Along the field, there were a few spots where you could hide: the garden wall, a few bushes and hedges, and the rubbish bin. I did not notice the abandoned locker rooms at first. They were overgrown with ferns and weeds. The locks were rusty and most of them unusable. How could I ever guess Silvius would be so stupid to lock himself up inside one of them?

"Are you in there? Come on, get out! I got you!"

"Matt, can you hear me? I can't re-open the lock. The handle is stuck! Please help me. Open it from the outside!"

My fingers froze the very moment I raised my hand to grab what was left of the handle from my side of the door. Instinctively, I stepped back and did not move an inch. A smile enlightened my face.

I turned and walked to the field where he had put the balloon to "rest". His screams sounded almost muffled through the door. On that sunny day, the stagnant, sultry heat was their perfect sounding board. I picked up the balloon and walked home, whistling.

Silvius was found on the fourth day. From that moment on, my mom is always sticking a bottle of water into my soccer bag. She doesn't want me to go out and play when the sun is so blazing hot.

Silvius' mother has not said hi to me since that day. Eventually, she and her husband moved to another town.

Rails

Glasgow Central Railway Station looked like a giant, seething cauldron: people running to catch trains, people buying tickets, people waiting for cabs or talking on the phone.

Youssouf stopped exactly in front of the huge ticket office, sniffing the air and trying to decrypt the mechanical buzz that was announcing arrivals and departures. He could not "chew" English very well yet. Studying it at school would be another kettle of fish. Suddenly, he thought he caught the word "*dilèi*" in the midst of sounds the metallic voice was reeling off. He pulled a little dictionary out of his pocket and began browsing it in search of a possible meaning.

He looked around, turning in place. He smiled at an elderly woman when her bag spilled open onto the floor, but he did not move to help her. For one moment, he envied the child who was choosing some postcards from the rotating support in the newspaper stand, as his dad looked at him with tenderness and patience. Youssouf's dad had never bought him a postcard in his whole life.

After that, he froze, staring at the big clock of the station. When the minute and the hour hands reached both the twelve, he closed his eyes and started praying.

"Allah is great."

A second later, he pushed the red button on the little detonator he was hiding in his right hand.

Dinner is ready!

Mrs. Gwendolyn had cooked the pot roast like every other Sunday. On that particular day, she prepared it with an almost maniacal, fawning care. It was meant for a very special occasion.

She set the table with the same attention. She arranged the linen napkins so that they would sprout from the wine glasses. She pulled the silver cutlery out of drawers and lined up the salad forks precisely next to the steak knives.

"Dinner is ready. Take a seat!" She announced pompously, coming out of the kitchen with a tray in her hand.

She cut the portions for her two children and sat down herself. She poured wine in her husband's glass and hers, too, but she did not drink it or even taste it. She tried a piece of roast and allowed herself a moan of satisfaction when it caressed her palate. Keeping her eyes closed, almost without chewing, she let the beef gently slip from over her taste buds down her throat.

She roused only when Hugo's forehead slammed noisily onto the plate in front of him.

"Mom? What's wrong with dad? Is he sleeping?"

"Your father was a pervert. Keep this in mind when they take you away from me."

"Who? Why? Are you going to leave?"

Mrs. Gwendolyn did not reply. She stood up, took the bottle of wine and the two glasses and hurried to empty them down the kitchen sink. At the same time, she turned the faucet to maximum force.

"Finish your food or it will get cold!" She ordered the boys, overpowering the noise of water with her voice.

Master & slave

It's time to bring this to an end. I can't stand him anymore. He laid the last affront on me yesterday night: by using my tongue, he forced me to clean the spot where an oil drop had accidentally fallen onto the floor.

He has been holding me captive in this house – our parents' house – for years by now. He killed them when he realized they knew he was a psycho. He holds me tied to a chain all day long; when he comes back home, he makes me wear an apron and orders me to cook for him, and to serve him as his personal slave. I have to fall down on my knees and kiss his feet. If I were not to do that, he would kill me.

We are exactly alike.

Before killing our parents, he pretended to go abroad. He remained there for a few months and I thought he would never come back. He let me know he got married. Definitely, he was a hell of a liar.

One night, out of nowhere, he came back without notice. I helped him make the bodies disappear. I called the police myself to report our parents were missing. Nobody ever found them so the case was closed after some hypocrite announcement on TV, which didn't achieve any effect by the way.

My personal nightmare started that very day. I am a weak man; I do not have the strength to fight back because he... he is my master.

I don't even have the will to live. I am powerless and at his mercy. He orders, I obey. Every single day, he makes up a new way to mortify me or a new excuse to beat me. Then, after beating me up, he starts indulging me; he says I am his beloved little brother; he says he doesn't get how he could have hurt me; he promises it won't happen again.

He even heals me, caressing me the way a bad mother would, as I cry for the pain.

This must come to an end. Tonight, when he comes back home, I will kill him and then I will fly far away from this city. I don't know where yet.

I need to free myself. But how? I do not have the nerve to do that. I am an incapable man, a loser. I need him.

I need hiiiiim.

What is it? They are calling out for me. I think because it's interview time. How boring! Interviews really suck. The nun who is to interview me has a stinky breath, and so does my cellmate.

I want to stay here; I don't want anybody to interview me. They said I have a personality disorder. Me? They have a personality disorder. I'm fine.

They have a personality disorder. I'm fine.

They have a personality disorder. I'm fine.

They have a personality disorder. I'm fine...

Flight AA11

"Hello? Can you hear me?"

"American Airlines Reservations office. Who is speaking?"

"This is Samantha Warren, attendant on flight AA11 from Boston to L.A. We've been hijacked!"

"Repeat that, please. We can't hear you... Where are you calling from?"

"From the phone at the bottom of the plane. They threw us out of first class and entered the cockpit... oh God! They just stabbed my colleague! Are you still there? Hello?"

"Yes, ma'am. Tell us who entered where and how many of them are there."

"I don't know, four maybe five... wait, wait... Oh no! One of them is in first class; he's wearing a bomb around his waist... three other men have entered the cockpit. Our captain is not answering the phone..."

"Calm down, Samantha. Do you remember where they were sitting? Were they first class passengers?"

"Yes, seats 2A and 2B. They just stood up after the take-off and stabbed our steward..."

"*Cuuuut!*" – The director shouted, losing his temper – "Brittany, I'm paying you out two million dollars; what about putting some passion in this? Damn it! You're on a plane that has just been hijacked! What about empathizing with your character, huh? It looks like you have a stick up your ass! Ten minutes break, then we're going to shoot it again!"

By Germano Dalcielo:

Jesus: A Hell of a Secret

It was pitch dark, an almost unnatural black. His eyelids felt like boulders, his mouth was completely dry and his neck was aching.

What the hell...?

Brother Raymond's first instinct was to breathe, just to expand his lungs. Unfortunately, only a weak, hoarse gasp came to his throat.

Something slimy stuck to his nostrils. He moistened his lips and his tongue returned an earthy flavor of something plastic. He tried to raise his arm to his face, but it felt like raising a bag of cement. When his right hand rubbed against a moist and gritty pellicle, he opened his eyes in sudden realization.

A horrifying scream froze in his throat. He had no saliva.

Oh Father Almighty! I am buried alive...

Hooked?
Want to know Jesus' dirty little secret?

Acknowledgements

We really need to thank the German artist, Markus Lovadina, for drawing the cover image.
Last but not least, thanks to You, Reader, for choosing these stories.

About the authors

In October 2008, Germano Dalcielo published "*Il gene dell'azzardo*" (The gambling gene), a short autobiography about his gambling addiction in 2000-2006.

In 2010, he wrote "*Il segreto di Gesù*" (**Jesus: a hell of a secret**), an Italian best seller for three months in a row in the Kindle store.

In October 2011, he published a few short stories, "*Lettere dal buio*", available in English as **Darkness, come on in...**

Elvio Bongorino is the pen name of a female author that would rather remain anonymous.